BATTLE SCARRED LOVE

Author Y. Deonna

Cover designed by Thaiala Gardner

ISBN: 9781733058520

Author Y. Deonna
authorydeonna.wixsite.com/crownedbythecreator

Printed in the United States of America

Second Printing: May 2019
Crown Ruby Publishing

SYNOPSIS

This is a re-release formally titled This Kind of Love
Royale Chastain is the daughter of Virginia-based Bishop Grayling
Chastain and Christian reality show celebrity, Royce Chastain. She's the
quintessential preacher's kid. She's beautiful, poised, intelligent and a
philanthropist. She works in the community, is a mentor to the young girls
attending her church and is working on an international non-profit to end
child marriages.

So, what could possibly go wrong?

At twenty-three, she's ready to settle down with the love of her life, Matan.
He is her happily ever after until an act of betrayal causes her to walk away
from everyone. Her faith is tested, her life a complete mess, and family
destroyed. Feeling crushed, her anxiety attacks resurface, and she feels lost
and alone. She wants to give up until she meets him.

Khan Masterson is from West Virginia and owns his own business. He has
survived his mother's murder and is doing his best to rise above the stigma
that has attached itself to him ever since his father became a Klan member.
Even though his father is participating in activities he doesn't agree with,
they still live together because Khan feels it's his duty to help his father,
who suffers from a medical condition. He accepts life as it is until he meets
what could be his forever.

One night, on a dark road, he meets the one woman who can change his
entire world for the better. She is beautiful, broken, and Black, yet she is
everything he needs. However, love is never easy, love is a battle. As the
two grow closer, their relationship is challenged by their pasts. Will their
love be able to survive, or will they succumb to the hate and distrust that

threatens their love?

CHAPTER 1

May 2015

Royale's entire body trembled in wanton anticipation, as she closed her eyes to calm her anxiety. Tonight, was the night. The night before graduation, she was about to give herself, her body, to her longtime boyfriend and future husband, Matan. It would be the first time for them both, and she wanted it to be special. Jitters had almost gotten the best of her, and sweat covered her hands like gloves, but before her nerves could overtake her, she remembered the pep talk her best friend and cousin, Czarina, had given her. It provided her the boost she needed. At twenty-three, soon to be twenty-four, they'd waited long enough. They'd been together since her sophomore year of high school, but back then, they were friends. Being the bishop's kid, there were certain expectations and limitations she made sure to adhere to, but now, she was ready.

As she ascended the steps to his third-floor apartment, she pulled out her key. She hoped he didn't mind her coming over unannounced. If he did, once he saw what her curvaceous, size twelve frame was holding, which was some very expensive lingerie, he'd be all over her. She put her key in the door and pushed it opened. As soon as she entered, her nose was assaulted by a musty smell, and her ears were attacked by loud screams and moans. Just like that, her stomach dropped to her feet like she was on the Tower of Terror she got on when her family had taken a vacation to Disney World. Something wasn't right, but her mind wasn't ready to admit what it could be because Matan would never be unfaithful to her. There had to be a better explanation.

She knew Matan had some wild friends who liked to use the apartment as their own playground. Even though Matan complained before about their mannish actions, the activity continued. She hoped they were all in Fontaine's room because she didn't want them to know what she was about to do. However, she was sure she hadn't noticed any car that belonged to the wild bunch, or his roommate, Fontaine, in the parking lot. Flipping her long, dark chocolate hair over her shoulder, she moved. Although her feet felt like cement, she compelled herself to move forward and investigate.

Without even knowing what she was about to see, tears stung her honey copper eyes. She choked as her heartbeat increased tenfold. The beating was so intense, she momentarily forgot how to breathe. She moved onward, and once she passed Fontaine's door, she knew the sounds were of Matan and someone else. If there was any doubt, a female voice was humming his name like she was singing a church hymn solo. Straight soprano!

Royale's breath hitched as she cautiously opened the door. Her lips moved with no words coming out as she prayed. It took a moment for her mind to comprehend what she was witnessing. The obscene vision was too awful to be true. There was no way this was happening. She shook her head, hoping the image would change and the smell would evaporate, but there was no mistaking what she saw.

Like a fool, she watched in silent horror. She watched the man she had loved her entire life in bed with her mother. Her mother! She was stunned stupid. Her body began to tremble and her eyes watered, but the tears refused to fall. They, too, were stunned by betrayal. Her pulse thumped so loudly, she could hear and feel it. Was she about to have a heart attack? Was she dying? It sure felt like it as her body started to shut down. It felt like ocean waves were roaring in her ears, and her veins felt like pure blue fire was running through them. She was hot, like volcanic lava hot. Sweat broke out on every visible part of her body, and she teetered back and forth, trying to make sense of the awful scene.

Somehow, she found her voice, though it was small and full of anguish. "Mom?" she called out, still wishing with all her might that it was just a hallucination, but her mother's head popped up, and

Royale's red cinnamon eyes clashed into unforgiving sable ones and she knew it was no illusion. That was her mother with her boyfriend— no, he was her ex now. How could they? Why? What had she ever done to deserve this?

"Babe...baby, let me explain," Matan offered.

She wanted to scream and shout, but instead, her world went black.

"Ma'am, ma'am, please wake up, we're deplaning."

Royale could vaguely hear a voice in the distance. Her mother and Matan...together. Was she still dreaming? No, she finally concluded as gentle hands and a soft-spoken voice continued to persuade her to awaken. Several seconds later, she opened her eyes and saw a smiling flight attendant. Then, she looked around her surroundings and noticed everyone else had deplaned.

Widening her eyes, she apologized to the attendant and then hopped out of her seat and reached for her carry-on before exiting the plane. Sleep used to be peaceful, but now, it had become just as stressful as life. She hated to sleep because her mind always replayed the past, and even in her dreams, she lost her first and only love. The situation had haunted her since she left and went to Nairobi, Kenya. Every single night for eight weeks, her mind was invaded by that vile image.

As she entered the airport, she noticed the rain and how dark gray the sky was, practically a perfect representation of her depressed and darkened heart. The entire situation had taken a toll not only on her but also on her relationship with God. She was angry and hurt.

Two months ago, she walked in on the love of her life, Matan Haddon, in bed with her mother, the First Lady of Holy Trinity Inter-Faith Worship Center. Her mother, the woman who ministered to street women and held birthing classes for underaged mothers, was a harlot. That, she could have forgiven over time, but the fact that her mother was in bed with the man she planned on marrying was unforgivable. Feeling deeply deceived and abandoned, Royale skipped college graduation and hopped on a plane to do a Christian mission in Nairobi. For eight weeks, she buried herself in sharing God's word with children and their families, all the while harboring the vilest of feelings against her vessel, which was the term she used when speaking of her mother. She adored her once, and now she borderline despised her.

For eight weeks, she repressed her agony and refused to feel. It was too much, the loss too great, and she was dealing with it alone. It seemed to always be that way. To save herself, she detached from everyone except her Aunt Gwendolyn, who she had referred to as Ma ever since she could remember, and her first cousin but more like a sister, Czarina.

Czarina was Gwendolyn's daughter and only child. Royale expected one, if not both, to pick her up and take her home, and by home, she meant with Ma Gwendolyn, not with her father, Bishop Grayling Chastain. She was upset with him as well. Through her cousin, she found out that her father was standing by his adulterous wife and had sent her off to rehab for her sex addiction.

It was all a pile of crock and everyone knew it. That woman didn't have a sex addiction, she had a self-absorb addiction. Then again, First Lady Royce Chastain, daughter of gospel great Patty Royce and retired Army General, a friend of Gen. Colin Powell and longtime politician Sen. Eli Peterson, could do no wrong. Not only that, she was in the third season of the hit reality show, First Ladies of DC, even though she lived in Fairfax, Virginia. Royce had become the NeNe Leakes of the show, also known as the head lady in charge. Even though it was supposed to be a Christian show, it had the same ratchetness, gossiping, and backstabbing as any other reality show. The women were loud, too proud, came off bitter at times, and then acted like the biggest saints every Sunday. It was scandalous.

The only reason Royce was in rehab was because she didn't want to lose her paycheck or position on the show, which Royale never wanted to be part of. She hadn't renewed her contract. She'd only done the previous seasons at Royce's request. She was done. That life was gone, and Royce's excuses didn't matter to Royale. No one could excuse the behavior of her forty-eight-year-old mother seducing a much younger, twenty-four-year-old Matan. In her mind, that was too much for even reality television. However, she soon found out that the network was eating it up and ratings had gone through the roof. So sad. They made money off her misery.

After ambling through the airport, looking and feeling more zombie-like than human, she finally retrieved her suitcase from baggage claim. Thankfully, no one took notice of her. She would die a thousand deaths if she heard 'aren't you that girl?'. Sighing, Royale headed out the sliding doors, seeking either Ma Gwendolyn or Czarina. She turned left and then right, shielding her face from the torrent rain that was falling hard and heavy, obstructing her view. Giving up her attempt to see through the gray fog, she pulled out her iPhone and mumbled to herself because she had forgotten to turn it back on. Waiting for it to power up, she remembered she had changed her number, and she hadn't told anybody what it was. She hoped they picked up when she called.

Her mental narrative was interrupted by a recognizable, accented cadence, one she hadn't heard in months, but knew well. She glanced up to see him. He'd transformed, at least physically. He had lost a few pounds and muscled up a bit, but that fit his five feet eleven inch frame. No longer did he have the slight roundness to his belly, which was the first thing she noticed. The second was his face. He was always well groomed but gone was the beard and mustache combo and left were a clean-shaven face and a bald head. Then she noticed his eyes, they were strained, ebony eyes, with just a hint of baggage underneath. He still had that powerful aura and intimidating gaze, but it didn't affect her as it once did. No, she had lost respect for her father. He chose to side with his wife and not his daughter, and in her mind, that was the end of it. He couldn't have it both ways. Either he was on her side and would leave Royce to stew in her own mess, or he would support his daughter; there was no room for being lukewarm. She shouldn't be surprised that the only other man in her life had chosen Royce as well. He could rot right with her. The entire time she had these thoughts, she just stared at her father, never blinking or speaking, but she was sure he'd heard everything she thought.

"Sweetheart, I know you requested my sister or Rina to pick you up, but I wanted to be the one to get you. We have so much to discuss, and you ran off without so much as a goodbye after everything happened," he started.

Rina was short for Czarina. Yeah, their parents had gone a little overboard on naming their daughters like they were royals. Believe it or not, when they were younger, Royce termed them "the Royals". Totally classless, but that was Royce, always over the top. "I'm sorry you drove all the way out here to Dulles International Airport, but I'm not going back to your home. I've discussed my arrangements with Ma Gwendolyn via Skype. If she can't come get me, I can take a taxi." She didn't miss the aggrieved look on his deep colored molasses face. However, it wasn't her place to make him feel comfortable when she wasn't the one at fault. Nope, her days of being a dutiful daughter were over.

"Look, Roycee, I know you–"

She cut him off, shaking both her head and index finger. He had no right to address her as Roycee; it was too close to her vessel's name. Roycee was once a pet name she reveled in because she adored that woman at one time, but no more. There was no love left in her being for that woman. She had betrayed her trust for the last time. "Please, do not speak that horrid pet name ever again, and don't even attempt to suggest that you know how I feel. I assure you, you don't. I don't want to be crude or maliceful, but I have no desire to participate in a conversation that pertains in any way to your wife. I'll just hail a taxi." She ended their conversation abruptly and turned her attention to an awaiting taxi. She didn't get far before her father reached out and pulled her back with a strength she didn't know he had.

She was forced to face him, and his eyes had darkened and his face hardened. She knew her father didn't appreciate her tone or attitude as it was contradictory to her character. However, the person she used to be had died that night when she witnessed the worst treachery. She let out a calming breath as her father eased his grip on her upper arm.

"You're emotional and feel betrayed. So, I'll allow you a moment, starting now, but in the next five minutes, you'll get in the truck and I will take you home. Once home we'll converse responsibly and respectfully about our next steps."

For some reason, that only incited her ire more. That displeasure she was attempting to dominate, and control took over. She jerked from her father's grasp, more than likely causing a scene, but she didn't care. She wasn't just emotional, as he so incorrectly presumed, she was broken, dismantled, undone and lost. She was decaying inside because she had done everything right, and still, her forever fairytale was ripped from her. "If you think I'll set foot in a house where that harlot lives, offering the red light special, then you know nothing about me." She watched with satisfaction as her father looked aghast and paled at the slight she'd addressed his wife with. That satisfaction was short-lived when her father, the bishop, slapped her taste buds clear to Canada. Her neck snapped so hard, she thought she had whiplash.

Alarmed and perplexed by his violent response, she touched her face where her father had hit her to ease the sting and to ensure her bruised cheek was still attached to her face. Her father had a distressed expression on his face, as if his reaction had surprised him too. She didn't care. She simply gathered her luggage to retreat. Her face and mouth were throbbing, but she gaited quickly to a cab that another passenger was exiting. She didn't even look back as her father called her name. There was nothing to say.

"Where to, Miss?" the driver asked after putting away her luggage.

Royale spat off her aunt's location, then sat back as the tears started to fall. The sadness and shame hit her all at once. She wanted to curl into a ball and disappear.

"Miss, I see what happened. I call the police and I'll be witness for the assault," the driver offered. His accented voice sounded melodic to her ears, even though his English was broken.

The pitiful look on his face embarrassed her more. She didn't need pity, though she was sure she looked pitiful. "No, that won't be necessary."

"Miss, you bleeding. My wife works at shelter for women like you. I not mind helping. If he hit you once, he do it again."

Bleeding? She touched her lip and saw that he was right. She was only bleeding because of her braces, which were coming off in a few months. Shaking the thought, she rolled her eyes. This man thought her father was her boyfriend. He was freaking fifty years old, and though he didn't look it, he did appear too old to be mistaken for her man. She laughed at that absurd notion. "That was my father. I guarantee you he'll never hit me again." That was a promise. No matter what she said, he didn't have the right to hit her. There was no coming back from that.

The driver shook his head, but the rest of the drive was completely silent, as she looked out the window, watching it rain. The thought came back again, replaying like a Ferris wheel. Her father had hit her, her vessel had an affair with her now ex, and she was the one who felt the guilt and shame. It was time to leave the state of Virginia. There was nothing here for her anymore.

She was glad she had applied to graduate schools out of state. The DMV area had great schools and great programs, but she needed to go where no one knew her or her over the top, famous family. It was a surprise that her father could be at the airport without some TMZ reporter or some other entertainment news following him. His church had served as a place where many top politicians, even the President, had visited, and he was the son-in-law of Patty Royce. Then his wife, who was in the center of a scandal, was the head first lady on a popular reality show. After Royce's perfidy, the entire incident made it to national news level, more than likely because people loved to see Christians fall. There was this misconception that non-Christians had, believing Christians thought they were walk-on-water perfect. Sadly, her mother really did give off that vibe on the show, but how the mighty fall. From what Czarina shared, the paparazzi had descended like jackals to a lion kill. However, to her knowledge, there were no cameras or reporters to record what her father had done. Good, because the last thing she needed was to be back in the center of the media.

"Miss, we're here."

Here? Royale had missed the entire drive due to being so lost in her own thoughts. Shaking it off, she thanked the driver, paid him with a tip included, and asked if he had the information about his wife's shelter. Royale had a soft spot in her heart for women and children who were surviving domestic and sexual violence. Ma Gwendolyn had been a victim of abuse, well, survivor, because the word victim had such a negative connotation to it. She knew when Gwendolyn saw her face, she was going to be livid with her brother Grayling for putting it there.

The driver, who she found out was named Alim, wrote down the information and she thanked him, then she turned and sauntered toward Gwendolyn's home. Finally, the rain had eased, but her hair had been ruined a long time ago since she had no umbrella. She chided herself as she ambled to the house, and before she could knock, Rina ran out with an umbrella and puffy eyes. That meant her father had already called and most likely confessed his sin to his younger sister. Ever since the departure of Czarina's father, Royale's dad had stepped to the plate as a dad, which was why the two were more like sisters than first cousins. Royale's father stepped up in her life, and Rina's mother stepped up in Royale's life because her mother had better things to do. First lady work was demanding. Yeah, well, whatever.

As soon as Royale's eyes connected with Rina's, she started weeping all over again and Rina wrapped her in her arms. "I'm sorry, sissy."

They stayed enveloped in each other's embrace until Gwendolyn ushered them inside and instructed the butler to bring in the luggage. She encouraged Royale to sit on the loveseat that was in the living room before speaking to her. "Royale tell me what happened," Gwendolyn urged. "I have my brother's story, now I want yours. I want you to know that no matter what you tell me, my brother knows better than to react in violence. I'm infuriated and disappointed in his actions."

Royale nodded. She knew Ma Gwendolyn would be impartial. "Ma, he hit me. I know, I know, I can have a mouth on me when I'm ticked off. I was upset and surprised that he was picking me up. I'm not ready to have a conversation with him or his wife. I told him as much and that I wasn't going to a harlot's house. Then, he lifted his hand and slapped me so hard. My face is swelling, and I assume my lip is busted because they both hurt." She turned to let her aunt see the damage, and by her intake of breath, she knew there would be an ugly bruise.

"He should've never put hands on you. I told him I would pick you up, but he insisted. Your mother is in one of those intensive, ninety-day programs and has a month to go, so he wanted you to visit her with him. Apparently, she's at the phase where she needs to speak to the people she's hurt."

It didn't faze Royale one bit. Again, this was all for the reality show and had nothing to do with her love for her daughter. She wasn't ready and didn't know if she ever would be, but her aunt continued.

"Since this affair has been brought to light, it has had an impact on the church and the ministries. Your father has done his best to calm the flock and bring everyone back together. We lost some members. I think the stress of it all has deeply impacted him. I'm not excusing his reaction to your anger, but I doubt he was in his right mind. I've never known my brother to lift his hand in violence, only in praise."

"There's a first time for everything," Royale curtly replied.

"Sissy, Dad loves you. I know he didn't mean it," Rina added.

Royale gave a soft chuckle, borderline manic, before responding. "You said the same thing about your bio-father, and we know how that ended."

"Royale!" Gwendolyn castigated, before reaching out to her bereaved daughter. "Royale, I'll not tolerate that from you. I understand your pain, but I'll not accept such profane insolence in my home. You know we don't speak of him. We love you, but that impious attitude and acrimony in your heart are not welcome here."

Her aunt was right, she was being sarcastic and downright rude. It was the pain speaking. That was a low blow, but it was true what they say: misery loves company, and she was lonely and miserable. It didn't help that Ma Gwendolyn and Rina were defending her father's actions, knowing that they came from an abusive situation. No, she wasn't comparing her father's act of rage to the horror her aunt and cousin had suffered, but it scared her all the same. Now she regretted coming back home. She should have extended her stay in Nairobi. There she had a purpose; here she had to face her problems, and she was too bitter to admit that truth. "You're right. I apologize. It's not either of your faults that I'm a discombobulated mess. If you don't mind, I'll shower and be on my way."

"Honey, I'm not asking you to leave. I'm just saying you have to start healing and you can't heal by hurting those who love you."

"Yes, ma'am. However, I'm not prepared to be around family. I know this now, so, as I said, I'll shower and be on my way." Then she got up, sick to her stomach for some reason, but she managed to get to the bathroom before vomiting airplane snacks. The putrid taste of acid clung to her tongue, so she brushed until her gums bled. It stung because the inside of her lip was split as well, but she didn't stop. Then she got in the shower and let her tears mix with the water.

◆ ◆ ◆

Grayling couldn't believe he had hit his daughter. He didn't even spank her as a child, yet he had hit her. He ministered to men who did that, he helped women who needed to get out of abusive relationships like that. Here he was, hitting his own daughter because he couldn't handle the truth. Her trust had been violated by her mother's and Matan's selfish actions, then he added insult to injury by hitting her.

All of this stemmed from his wife's need to be famous, her overindulgence of self, and lack of respect for her own family. Her affair was blasted all over the news. He never wanted to be on a stupid reality show anyway, which in his mind, was the downfall of his marriage. He let his wife influence his decision, and all he could think about was Adam, Eve, the serpent and Eve eating the forbidden fruit. Just like them, he had failed, and it was tearing him up inside. He was a man of God and had reacted like a man of the world. That look on her face, the pain in her honey eyes, he would never be able to get that out of his mind. She didn't deserve that. It wasn't his daughter who he was angry with, it was his wife. He had wrongly taken his frustration out on his daughter, the only one innocent in the entire mess.

After calling his sister and confessing his sin, she ripped him a new one, as she should. Now, here he was, parked outside her home in Williamsburg. It was on the northern edge of Arlington County, along the Fairfax County line, which was where he lived. He let out a sigh as he got out of his truck. His sister had called him back and explained that Royale planned to leave her house after a minor spat that left a sensitive Rina in tears, and his daughter feeling like she had no one in her corner.

Loneliness could be a destroyer, especially when going through a trial like she was. Another sigh. He had gone about this all wrong.

Royale needed him, and all he could think about was himself. Shaking the guilt, he inhaled a deep breath and exhaled it as he walked to his sister's door. He knocked once and was greeted by Gwendolyn. He gave his sister a once over, and it looked like the ordeal had left her a little tattered. Her eyes were puffy, and there was redness around her nose. She was barely five feet five, but there was a lot of wisdom, fierceness, and forgiveness in her. Though she was his younger sister, she kept him straight.

"Gwendolyn, are you all right? Is the situation direr than you told me over the phone?" he questioned, concerned.

She nodded before speaking. "Grayling, I'm still ticked that you slapped your daughter. Half her face is swollen, her lip busted, and her feelings are fragile. You need to apologize for the physical damage you caused, but I'm extremely concerned about her mental state. She isn't herself.

"When we talked while she was in Nairobi, she had a bit of a sparkle. Albeit, we never discussed what led her there, but right now, that young woman who entered my house is a stranger. She's lost. I don't know if your presence will be viewed as relief or as agitation, but she needs us."

Grayling dropped his head at her admonishment and concern, as his sister retold what had happened when his daughter arrived at her house. He sat back on the sofa and nodded his thanks to Rina as she brought him a beverage. He had an affinity for Bai drink, something his girls, meaning Rina and Royale, had gotten him hooked on. All part of their 'get Dad fit' campaign. The sad truth was, it was his wife's infidelity that had gotten him into shape. Her actions made him insecure, and he hit the gym, hard. In his mind, she had cheated because he had let himself go and gotten too comfortable. He never really thought about his appearance. Women often told him he was attractive, but his mind had always been on serving the Lord. Maybe if he had put more effort into his family and his appearance, maybe… He let the thought drift unfinished as Rina's voice interrupted.

"Dad don't worry. Sissy is going to be okay. We just need to remember that she witnessed something terrible, fainted, missed her graduation and hopped on a plane to Nairobi. She never got to process or get any of her questions answered. Her pain has festered and spread, so we have to be cognizant of her feelings," Rina lectured.

Grayling was so proud of Rina. For five years, she was mute because of the violence she had witnessed her biological father put her mother through. Now, she was in her senior year of college, top of her class, and following in Royale's footsteps of being a Rhodes Scholar. His girls were the cream of the crop: beautiful, intelligent, well-educated, black, Christian women. Any parent would be proud of half of what they had accomplished, all while doing missionary trips and giving back to the community. Now he had to get Royale back on track. He wasn't sure what her plans were since she had graduated, but he hoped he and her mother's mistake hadn't dampened her ambition and put her in a hole so deep, he couldn't reach.

They were all talking, when Royale's sweet timbre interjected the leisure conversation. "Sissy, can I speak to you for a moment?"

Grayling watched as Rina got off the couch and quickly sauntered toward Royale. It was then he saw only a glimpse of her swollen face and lip, making his heart lurch and breath halt. He had done that. After her mother had mentally abused her by her selfish deed, he had physically wounded her for only telling the truth. Now he was sure by the way his daughter avoided his direct gaze that he had lost her. That was the last thing he ever wanted to do. He needed her just as much as she needed him, but his betrayal was still fresh, and her body language told him she wasn't ready.

"You all, I'll be right back. Sissy and I are going out," Rina turned and told them.

"Will you two be back for supper?" Gwendolyn asked, as Grayling quietly monitored the situation.

Rina played with her fingers. Grayling knew that was a tale; something more had been debated between them. He was sure of it but permitted the scene to play out. If he said anything now, it could make the current mood explode. Besides, both girls were adults, so he couldn't forbid them from doing anything. He just prayed whatever they had discussed, wouldn't get either of them hurt.

"Um, I'm not sure, momma. Probably not."

Gwendolyn and Grayling nodded and watched the two left the house. Grayling did note that the only bag Royale had was her purse. That made him hopeful that she had changed her mind and would be staying at his sister's house.

CHAPTER 2

"Royale, you don't have to leave," Rina pleaded. Her large green eyes watering in concern.

"Yes, I do. People recognize me here, and I can't deal right now. Take me to my car. I have my car keys, and I'll follow you back. I'll load up my belongings since you so expertly moved all my stuff from the bishop's house. Believe me, it's necessary that I get out of here."

Royale didn't want to go too deeply with her cousin. She knew Rina was sensitive, and she didn't want to upset her further. She needed to leave. It was imperative to her mental and physical health that she exited Virginia as soon as possible.

"Go where? I need to know where you're going."

"Somewhere." Royale was keeping her location secret. She didn't want to be found like she had been in Nairobi. She watched as Rina sucked her teeth and shook her head. The action allowed her honey blonde locks to swing free in the wind. "This is so uncharacteristic and irresponsible of you. All our family is in the DMV area. Please believe your Dad will send out the freaking National Guard to find you, not to mention the General. Both nearly lost their mind when you disappeared and went to Nairobi, unbeknownst to anyone. Dad thought you'd committed suicide or something crazy like that."

Royale gave Rina a dubious glare. She was laying it on Eucerin lotion thick. True, her heart had been shattered, even her soul was damaged, but she was not and never had been suicidal or homicidal. If the bishop thought she was, then they were more disconnected than she had previously presumed. Just like her mother was caught up in her reality show, her father was caught up in being the next T.D. Jakes. He was all over the world, bringing the gospel, but forgetting about his family...forgetting about her. Some stuff had occurred that he never knew about because he wasn't there. Quickly removing those dark memories, she turned her attention back to Rina, who looked as though she had lost her best friend.

"Sweet Czarina, I honestly doubt the bishop will anguish over my departure. He didn't welcome me with open arms when I returned.

Instead, I was greeted with a violent slap to the face." She paused and pointed to her current disfigured state before continuing. "It's safe to say my arrival is unwanted, and believe me, I don't care. Now, be a good sister and say nothing. I'm an adult. I don't need anyone's approval about my travel. I'll be in touch. Now, just follow the plan."

Royale was aware that Rina didn't like it. She wore all her emotions on her face, but Royale also knew Rina had her back after Grayling had slapped her. Royale firmly believed her Rina would do as instructed. It seemed that fate was on their side because when they returned to the house in Arlington, both Gwendolyn and Grayling were gone. That made it easy for them to load as much as they could into Royale's candy painted red SUV.

"I love you, big sis. I wish you weren't leaving. However, I think I understand that you need a moment to relax, reset, and regain your balance as you work through everything. Just call me. If you miss a call, I'll go straight to our parents and the General and sell you out like a snitch looking at life."

Royale laughed. It felt so good to laugh. She did love Rina. "I won't miss a call. You have my word on that. Best friend, I'm sorry about that crude remark I made. I had no right to bring *him* up."

"It's okay. I know you didn't mean it. That was the hurt talking. We're best friends, cousins, sisters, and there isn't anything you can say or do that I won't forgive."

At that, Royale reached for Rina and pulled her into a tight hug. It took all her effort not to cry. "Rina, me too, even if you snitch on me. I love you. I'll keep in contact. I just need to leave so I can breathe, think and move forward. Right now, I can't heal here. There's too much baggage."

"Go before the parents get back. I love you," Rina replied and watched her sister go, blowing her a kiss as she got into her SUV to leave.

◆ ◆ ◆

Before starting out on her trip, Royale made a stop at Starbucks. It was her favorite place to go. It was a luxury she had missed while in Nairobi. Her mouth was salivating for a vanilla bean drink and a chocolate croissant, maybe two since her stomach was empty. It didn't dawn on her until she entered that this was also where she and Matan would hang out, and sometimes have little dates between classes. It was a memory that hurt. It physically caused her head to throb, so she retreated from it. Honestly, being home was painful because there were memories everywhere. She didn't want to remember, but the more she fought it, the more it fought back.

Removing her rampant thoughts, she promptly got in line. Lucky for her, she had Starbucks gold status. That was how much of a Starbucks star she was. Royale made her order, and to her surprise the young woman at the register remembered her. Not good, because that meant she knew the scandal that was now attached to her family. However, instead of poking a badly unhealed wound, she simply smiled and said, "I'm praying for you."

Those simple words brought a sincere smile to Royale's face. "Thank you."

"You're welcome. You probably don't remember me, but my sister and I were homeless, and our mother had been abandoned by our abusive father when we made it to your church. My little sister was a mess. No one could calm her, but you. You sang *Love Psalm* to her and prayed over her until she fell asleep. Then you prayed with me."

That was when Royale looked at her shirt to see her name, Amelia, and her little sister was named Joanna. "I remember. The offer still stands for you to call me whenever you need. Let me give you my updated business card with my contact information," she offered.

Amelia smiled and thanked Royale before attending to the next customer. Royale moseyed over to the other side and patiently waited for her name to be called. When she heard her name, she thought that was amazingly fast, considering the three people ahead of her. Once her head snapped up, she was stunned to see Matan. Her irrational mind thought, *What was he doing here? This was her space.* Then, her rational mind took over. *Okay, so no, she didn't own it, but really, God, him? Anybody but him.*

Today wasn't going how she had planned. There he was, all tall and medium built, blemish free with a paper bag skin tone. He was clean shaven and by his shape up, he'd recently been to the barbershop. She used to love the smell of his hair after he'd been to the barbershop.

There was a time she loved everything about him. Now, his appearance made her feel nauseated.

He advanced her way with a slight limp that caused a laterigrade gait. It was from a childhood four-wheeling accident. Back in the day, it kind of added to his swagger. He made it work for him, but today, it wasn't. All those things that attracted her to him were gone. He wasn't handsome anymore. He wasn't her happiness anymore. Matan was nothing, and she had nothing to say to him. Royale narrowed her fire-lit eyes to warn him away because she didn't even want to waste her vocal cords on addressing him.

"I can't believe it's really you. I've been trying to contact you, but your number was disconnected. I emailed you, but you never responded. I even asked your mentee, January, if she heard from you." He looked her up and down before continuing. "I see you've lost weight, but I guess being in Nairobi can do that." Then he noticed her face and frowned. "What happened to your face? Are you okay? Talk to me, Roycee."

No, this mofo didn't just roll up with his unsmooth, no game, cheating with my momma, ain't saying sorry self and call me Roycee. How dare he ask me a million questions like he was part of the cast of Law & Order? How did he know my location? Why was he contacting January, which reminded her that she needed to check on her mentee, she thought before shifting her thoughts back to her ex.

He could sell that phony concern to the devil because she wasn't buying it. Everything in her wanted to crush him like he had crushed her heart. Her love for God wouldn't let her react violently, and she wasn't her father. Instead, she curved him and sauntered away as if he wasn't there.

"Roycee, sweetheart, please talk to me," he implored, loud enough to gain attention. That caused her instant embarrassment. By no means was she a timid woman, but she didn't like to draw unnecessary attention to herself—especially now. Rolling her eyes, she clamped her mouth down to refrain from shouting something she couldn't take back. Even though she was suffering, she was still a representation of God, her family, and her church. She would not falter.

Another customer, a man who had to be in his late twenties, approximately the same height as Matan and dressed in oversized clothing, asked if she were okay. "I will be if that man would leave me alone," she growled. Her think index finger pointed at Matan, irritation clear on her face.

The man shook his head. "Aye, homie, Ms. Lady said back off."

"Aye, homie, she's my girlfriend." Matan sarcastically mimicked the man's vernacular.

Royale whipped her head around and glared at Matan. The movement was painful due to her injury, but his lie hurt even worse. So, in her mind, she was giving it to him for old and new. However, the curses she was thinking didn't leave her lips. Instead, she shamed him. "No, we broke up the same night I found you in bed with my mother. I'm not your anything and never will be anything to you. Now back up off me you rock bottom vulture, or feel my wrath!"

"Ohh!" Some random people exploded.

"It's 'bout to get Jerry Springer crazy!" some other random person yelled out. "Did she call him a rock bottom vulture?" Now, everyone was looking, like, everyone. Starbucks stopped, *why*? Everyone knew the story, and now they had her jacked up face to go with it. It was bad enough to be bruised up, but then to have all the people looking at her was too much.

"Ms. Lady, you da one. Yo' momma that church lady on da show? I knew you looked familiar. You pretty!" he complimented before turning his attention toward Matan. "You's the clown who did it. You's a fool, my dude." Then he turned his attention back to Royale. "Man, Sweet Ma, you can do better. I'm Slow, and I can treat cha far better than that lame."

Royale shook her head. Did this man just introduce himself as Slow? There was no way his momma had named him that, and if she had, shame on her. This couldn't be life. No way in the world was all this happening in one day. She wished it was all a dream, but she was sure it wasn't. "Nice to meet you," she told him and shook his hand. Unlike Matan, she didn't judge people based on visual perception. To the human eye, Matan looked like the perfect specimen of a man, but he was a wolf in sheep's clothing.

"Royale, I know you aren't entertaining this buffoon in my presence. It's been two months." He put up two fingers to emphasize his point. "I thought you would have forgiven me by now, instead of trying to get some thug luvin'," he charged.

"Aye, homie, thugs need love too. You had yo' chance, and you chose the momma. I don't do cougars or married women. I'm faithful. So, honey love, the offer still stands if you looking for a new man."

While they argued, Royale saddled up to the counter and grabbed her order. She silently thanked the staff and then attempted to make a getaway but, today wasn't her day. At some point, people had started pulling out cellphones and were videotaping. Some of those said people were approaching her to ask questions. More than likely trying to get hits on IG, Twitter and Facebook at her expense. She had deactivated all her social media accounts because the trolls were ridiculous.

"Royale, I need to speak with you," Matan persisted.

"Back off, preppy, looking like a black Jonas brother. She'on want'cha holy roller whorishness on her like that, so leave."

"Nah, you back off, you Fetty Wap wannabe. She'll never be your trap queen, so go back to your side of town and leave me and mine alone."

"Nah, homie, she won't be yours again. Don't get mad because she wants to come my way. I'ma make her feel good with my trap luv. Take your L like a gangsta, you sissified church boy," Slow clapped back.

Then came the laughter and comments from outsiders, instigating the argument that didn't need to be happening in the first place. Royale wasn't interested in either of them. All she wanted was her snacks, and to leave.

Royale expelled a labored breath. This would have been a comical relief if it wasn't so embarrassing, and her heart wasn't beating out of her chest. Here was the usher board president's son calling another person out their name. Then insinuating said dude was a dope boy in search of a trap queen, all while quoting Fetty Wap lyrics. Times like these, she wished she had her bodyguards, but they went away when she did. She was doing her best not to have a breakdown.

Stay strong, she mentally chanted. She didn't want to have an anxiety attack, something that had started while she was in Nairobi. Something no one knew about. The last thing she needed to do was have an anxiety attack in front of strangers.

"C'mon, Royale, we'll get you out of here," Amelia offered, followed by two more employees who assisted her to her vehicle. They made sure to keep Matan at a distance as she drove away. She had nearly a five-hour drive to Charleston, West Virginia, where her sorority sister lived. She was headed towards I-68 W and I-79 S and would be there soon. She turned up Tye Tribbett on her iPod touch and let his voice fill her soul as she pushed out of her mind what had just happened. She was good at burying her pain and running away from her problems.

◆ ◆ ◆

"Where is she?" an aggrieved Grayling interrogated Rina. His solid frame dwindling at the thought of losing Royale again. They were back at Gwendolyn's house with his in-laws, Patty and Eli. They'd come once the internet exploded with Matan and some unknown quarreling and nearly coming to physical violence over Royale. It was all over the gossip blogs, Facebook live and entertainment news, but that wasn't why Grayling was worried. It was because his daughter's SUV was missing, and most of her clothing had been removed from the bedroom. That troubled him. She was upset and running. Something about her leaving this time felt permanent, and it concerned him greatly.

"Czarina, where's Royale?" The General's deep bass voice slashed through all the other questioning voices.

Grayling watched as Rina glanced at him, and then she looked at the General. Eli was an intimidating man. He stood 6'2", and even in his late sixties, he still had that Army persona. Not to mention, his hard, all-seeing eyes that could weaken the strongest man. Grayling was sure that if anyone could crack Rina, it would be him. He was too imposing a figure.

"I honestly don't know. She said she would check in with me, and she hasn't. In her defense, she said she needed some space to get her mind right."

"Why?"

"Well, sir, probably because over the last two months, she's had a double loss. Her mother and her boyfriend betrayed her."

He nodded, but she was taught to deal with her issues, not run from them. "What happened to her face?"

Grayling watched as she zipped up her lips and dropped her eyes to the floor. She was shutting down. Grayling suspired, and shared with his in-laws his moment of stupidity. Then just as he expected, Eli lit into him.

Grayling was worried about his daughter, and the fact that she ran into her ex, who clearly was trying to reunite with her. That wasn't happening. He didn't want Matan to have any interactions with her. He wasn't sure how much more she could handle before she flipped.

"Grayling, if anything happens to my grandbaby, I'll hold you personally responsible. Not even an army of angels will save you." With that threat, he got up from the table, kissed Rina, and paraded off with his wife following behind him in the same dramatic departure as their arrival.

"This is a disaster," Grayling groaned, collapsing in the chair that Eli had just vacated. It was still warmed by his body heat, which was needed since Grayling was having chills. Royale was out there alone, and nobody knew her exact location. He couldn't find her because she had her own phone plan and had changed her phone number in the eight weeks that she had been gone. Furthermore, she no longer had any active social media accounts, and apparently, even Rina didn't have her new cell number. He had to wait and be still, which was incredibly difficult to do when one's child was in a bad mental state.

"I'm sorry. I tried to stop her from leaving."

"It's not your fault, sweetheart. I did this. Now with God's instructions, I have to fix it." He knew why his daughter was still running. She wasn't ready, and he respected that, but he needed to know her location. He needed to know she was safe.

CHAPTER 3

Khan shook his head in dismay as he entered the bar that had become his father's favorite place to hang out since the death of his mother. That had been over a decade ago. He understood his father was troubled by the death, as was he, but he didn't turn to alcohol and abuse to cope. If that wasn't bad enough, he fell into the likes of white supremacists. Maybe he always felt that way, and his mother's murder only brought out the true beast inside his father. He wasn't sure.

His father, Ronald Masterson, was easy pickings after the high-profile murder case took over the state of West Virginia, and everyone had an opinion. It was all the talk that a Black thug, had murdered and sexually assaulted a Caucasian cop's wife in front of her son. He was the son, the only child. After his mother was murdered, life changed for him.

He was haunted by his mother's murder, but more so because he didn't recall it the way the lawyer presented the case, which was why he never testified. Medical professionals said he was in severe shock, and the therapist said he had blocked out the murder. Although sometimes, he got flashbacks, and the story in court and the one his father retold wasn't what he remembered. Life taught him to keep that to himself after his father had smacked him around.

The man who was arrested for the crime said he was innocent, swore to it, even after the all-white jury found him guilty. Just like that, his father, a now-retired police officer, took him out of school and homeschooled him. Ronald taught him that the white race was better, and to never mix with others. Asians were okay, but the muddies had to stay in their place. He told him to hate the man who had taken his mother, Khloe, but even to his adolescent brain, his father's philosophy didn't seem right.

Khan finally convinced his father to allow him to attend public school where he did the opposite of what his father had taught him. His mother never taught him to hate, but it was all his father spouted. He had grown sick of it. He would have left a long time ago, but his dad suffered from osteoarthritis, and he was a drunk, so he moved back into the trailer after college graduation to assist him. It was the worst decision he could have made. Hate and revenge had pretty much eaten away his dad's heart, just like the osteoarthritis was eating his joints.

"You here for the old man?" Teagan, the bartender, asked, unknowingly interrupting his narrative.

Khan nodded and followed Teagan's gaze. His father was out of it. Like seriously gone. He shook his head.

"Don't be too hard on him."

"Right. How much do I owe you?"

"It's all good. He's one of us. Just get him home in one piece."

Khan nodded but dropped forty dollars down on the bar anyway. He sauntered over to his drunk father and placed his large hand on his back to coax him awake. Once he had his attention, his father stumbled, but Khan assisted him in standing upright. The smell of beer and liquor breath lingered all over his body. It was a scent Khan had gotten used to smelling.

It was slow moving, as they left the bar and finally made it to the awaiting truck. Khan mentally berated himself for driving his larger truck because with his father's unsteady gait, he feared he may fall. That was all he needed.

Ronald had lost a lot of weight after the death of his wife, Khloe. He never gained it back, so maybe his concern was for nothing. Khan stood 6'6" and was about 257 pounds of muscle and had about four percent body fat. He was a big dude, but per his father, it was wasted on him because he was too soft. What that really meant was that he had no desire to participate in hate crimes or intimidate people based on their race or nationality. It was dumb. Hating people was stupid and a waste of time, but you couldn't tell his father that.

As a child, he really idolized his father, thinking he was a hero because he was a police officer. He wasn't as tall as Khan, he was 6'0" tall, and barely 180 pounds. Shaking his head, he got his father into the cab of the truck without issue. For a moment, he started to put him in the bed of the truck, just in case the old man couldn't hold his liquor but decided against it. It was getting dark, and the fool might actually hurt himself. Even though his dad was off, he was the only living parent he had. So…

After getting his dad situated, he jumped into the driver's side and took off. They were doing well. Ronald hadn't thrown up or acted irrational, and traffic was light. He turned up a Florida Georgia Line song bopping his head to the beat. He loved their music. He listened to a variety of music genres, but when in the presence of the old man, he kept it country, but even that was diversifying. One of his favorite songs was the Nelly and Tim McGraw collaboration, "Over and Over Again", and that Luda and Jason Aldean was fire too.

He settled in, nodding his head to the lyrics and humming along with it when he slammed on brakes to avoid hitting a stalled SUV. Whoever it was, didn't have their emergency flashers on. His dad's head jerked forward before he could react. He was thankful no one was behind him. His eyes locked with a very frightened woman. She was shaking.

Kham shook his head. What was she doing out here? Just as soon as he thought it, he saw her dilemma. The SUV wasn't stalled, she had a flat, or possibly a blown-out tire. It seemed she hadn't any idea what to do. The gentleman in him, the man his mother was raising him to become, wouldn't allow him to leave her unattended. He had to assist her.

Glancing at his father, he noticed he was still asleep. Good, because the woman he was about to help was a black woman, and he didn't want his father preaching his hate message.

Khan pulled his large, jacked-up diesel fuel truck behind her SUV. Yeah, he could be a real red neck country boy. He climbed out and strolled up to the woman.

"Hey, Miss, I'm Khan Masterson. I'm sorry for scaring you. I noticed you're in need of some help. I'm here to offer my assistance," he informed, offering her a sheepish grin. He hoped that would calm her discomfort because, right now, she looked terrified.

"I called the highway patrol."

He wasn't sure if she told him that because she feared him, or because she just thought it was helpful information, but he went with it. "Good, but until he or she arrives, let me assist you. No need to be scared, I won't hurt you. I promise. Do you have a spare?" he asked.

"I...I have an old tire. It was the best of the four I replaced."

"Even better. I can put it on for ya if that's all right. Oh, and Miss, turn on your four-way flashers. That's why I almost ran into the back of you."

She nodded. "Thank you." Then she dashed off like a skittish cat.

Just like that, he got to work, making small talk when he could, and found out her name was Royale. That was an extremely rare name, at least to him. Although, something about it was familiar, but he couldn't put his finger on it. She was from Virginia, he could tell by her license plate. After a while, she let down her guard and even offered him a bottled water, and he accepted.

"Royale, you should be good now. Just in case, let me hold your phone to put my number in so you can call me if you need any more assistance." He was surprised at how easy she offered her phone to him, but maybe it was because the highway patrolman had finally arrived. He did notice that someone had hurt her. It was on the tip of his tongue to ask, but he didn't want to pry.

Something was going on since she had what looked like her life's belongings packed in her SUV. Though one would adduce that by the swelling and bruising on her face, she was running from someone. The patrolman noticed too and gave him a look that he was quick to defend. He didn't hit women, ever. The woman in front of him was portrait pretty, and even though he didn't know her story, or her for that matter, he felt protective of her. He'd been like that since the night he failed to save his mother.

"Ma'am are you okay?" the patrolman asked.

"Yes, sir. Khan assisted me." Then she turned to Khan. "Thank you, Khan. May God bless your kindness. I'll be sure to pay it forward," she told him and reached for her phone. She thanked him and the officer again before getting in her SUV and leaving.

Khan bade the officer good night, then got back into his truck and headed home with his snoring father, who was doing a serious hog call. For some reason, his mind went back to Royale. She hadn't said much, but she had said enough. She was a gorgeous girl too. She had long, ebony hair, wholesome, honey copper eyes, a bright smile, and braces. He thought that was cute, but what caught him was that she wasn't toothpick thin. She could gain some more weight, but he liked her fullness. Like, he just knew she could kill it in the kitchen. He wasn't sure why he'd thought that, but he had. A man needed a woman like that. He also liked that she was Christian. While fixing her tire, he noticed she had a fish decal, and from what he could tell, she was in one of those Christian sororities, but there was something else about her, something familiar that he had yet to connect.

Parking his truck, he got out and was prepared to carry his father inside the house, but the old man picked that time to wake up and pop him on the top of his head.

"Pop calm down. No need for hittin', I was just assisting you. We're home. Teagan called me to come get'cha. I'll take you into town tomorrow to pick up your truck."

"Oh," was the only response Khan could get out of him, but at least he didn't go on a rant, as they walked into their single-wide trailer. As soon as his father entered the house, he headed to the fridge for a beer. Khan headed to the den to watch television. He flipped to the news because they didn't have cable, so there were limited channels. Khan was watching through hooded eyes until he saw *her*, the same her he had helped change a tire. Just like that, the connection he was trying to make was made.

She was the girl who'd caught her mom and boyfriend together, the same mom who was on that reality show. He had watched the reality show a few times when he had gone to visit his boy, Nehemiah. He shook his head in disbelief. That was Royale.

So, her ex-boyfriend had confronted her in Starbucks just a few hours ago, but it was unclear if he was the one who had physically attacked her. The funny part was the guy who had been deemed Fetty Wap, was now being interviewed. He confirmed that Royale arrived at Starbucks with her face already bruised, and to his knowledge, her ex-boyfriend hadn't been the one to do it, at least not in Starbucks.

"Turn that crap off. Them coloreds are so ignorant. You see how they treat each other. Out here shouting Black Lives Matter when a cop kills one of 'em, but silent when they attack each other. I swear they got to be the most backward people. They were better off being the white man's slave, at least then they knew their place. This country done gone to the dogs, and then they re-elect that Muslim, ISIL supporting, non-American as the president. All he did was show us they ain't equipped to run the country or lead their own lives without being told what to do. We need whites back in the White House and leave them coloreds to clean it. Yep."

Disgusted to the point of being physically ill, Khan clicked off the television and got up to leave. "Pop, I'm headed to a friend's house. I'll be back later." He was gone before his father could mumble goodbye. There was only so much of that obtuse rhetoric he could take. The man was a lost cause.

He hopped in his truck and headed to Nehemiah's house. If he were lucky, Ne's mom or sister might have cooked. He was in the mood for buttermilk biscuits. At the thought, he smiled and texted Nehemiah that he was coming over. He knew it wasn't an issue, even though it was past suppertime. He'd been doing it since high school, unbeknownst to his father.

When he pulled up, he honked his horn and Nehemiah opened the door and waved him in. He got out of his truck, his cowboy boots crunching the unpaved driveway. Once he made it to the front door, he knocked off the boots and walked in. When he entered, he took off his cowboy boots and hat, letting his long, dark blonde hair fall freely. He walked into the powder room to wash his hands because his next stop was the kitchen. A man his size could eat.

"The old man showing out?"

"You know it. What did Momma Byse cook?" he asked, not wanting to talk about his old man.

"Chicken dumplings, biscuits and a cinnamon roll cake."

"Not them Grands?" Khan asked, already getting excited at the idea of his favorite meal being fixed. That's why he loved Momma Byse. No matter the time, she had food ready.

"You know canned anything is scurrilous in this house."

Khan died laughing. It was that serious. Momma Byse made everything and shopped at the farmer's market or made her own food.

He didn't think she'd ever had fast food. The pair headed towards the kitchen.

"Khan, my sister's friend is in town. They oughta be back shortly, but just a heads up, she's kinda famous, so just be cool."

Khan nodded. He wasn't really bothered because the aroma coming from the kitchen had him hungry. He spoke to Momma Byse as she handed him a plate. He blessed his meal and then dug in. This was good cooking. All he needed was some greens, but he knew she'd fix some collard greens and cornbread Sunday as he ate with the family every Sunday.

"Ease up, bro. I promise nobody is going to take your plate," Nehemiah teased.

He smiled, showcasing his one dimple and bright white teeth, but didn't stop inhaling the food until his plate was clean, taking his biscuit, slopping up all the sauce and eating it. That was country boy eating.

"Good?"

Khan looked up at the sound of the feminine tone. It belonged to Nakisha, but everyone called her Kisha. Then he looked beyond her and saw Royale. Was she the famous friend? Oh, there is a God in heaven, he thought to himself. He was excited to see her again.

"Royale?"

Nakisha frowned. "How y'all…wait, is that Mr. Sexy Cowboy you were talking about?" Nakisha asked as she turned to look at a blushing Royale.

"Kisha, really?" Royale queried, embarrassed.

"What? That's Khan, he's like my other big brother. He ain't sexy, and he ain't a cowboy, he's just Khan. Don't give him a big head. He already thinks he's God's gift. The women go crazy over his size, height, and his long hair. It's the man buns that make the women melt," she joked.

Khan just laughed. So, Royale thought he was sexy. That was a compliment he could live with. Now he knew she was interested in him. "Kisha, what I told you about hating? Stop flexing on ya boy."

She laughed. "See? He's just showing out for you. He doesn't even know what flexing means. C'mon, hopefully, he left us something to eat."

"Kisha, be nice to your other brother," he jokingly admonished.

She sucked her teeth but smiled at him as she fixed her and Royale's plate.

"How's the tire?" he asked Royale as she sat down across from him.

"It's good. Thank you for asking. Um…about what Kisha said, I never said it like that."

He grinned. She was even prettier when she was embarrassed. Even with half her face bruised, she was still beautiful, and he loved that she had braces. It added to her innocence. "Aw, I was all excited, and now you just crushed me." Her honey eyes grew large, thinking she had really offended him.

"I'm sorry. I didn't mean to…it's just been a long day."

"I was only joking. I'm sorry. It was wrong of me. Do you want to talk about it?" he asked. It was evident something had happened to her, and he wanted to know what.

"Not with you," Kisha cut in. "She and I are going to talk because she's my friend and sorority sister. Don't you and Nehemiah have some game like Xbox or PlayStation to play?"

He shook his head and got up, cleaned off his plate and exited the kitchen in search of Nehemiah. He'd get to know Royale better, but now, she definitely needed a friend, and he respected that.

◆ ◆ ◆

After playfully chastising Kisha about calling her out to Khan, Royale finally started talking about why she'd shown up at her friend's house. Then she asked if she could stay for a week until her face healed, then she was headed to the University of Pennsylvania to start her graduate program, which was International Educational Development. She was in the beginning stages of creating her own nonprofit, Far Above Rubies, which was an organization to assist women in countries where child marriages were still performed. It was an idea she had gotten after meeting another young woman.

Even though school hadn't started yet, Royale planned to use the time before school to search for an apartment or condo that fit her needs, and then restart her life. Her original arrangement was to stay with Gwendolyn, but that was altered since there was just too much going on to stay in Virginia, and the stupid incident at Starbucks was stirring it all up again. If she went back home, she would more than likely have another anxiety attack, and she didn't need that. It was the sucking of Kisha's teeth that brought Royale back to the present.

"In one day, your dad, one of the most influential, well-connected and well-respected men of God, *the* Bishop Chastain, slapped the piss out of you. After which you to go to your aunt's house where he follows, but you two don't even acknowledge each other. Then you see your cheating ex-boyfriend at Starbucks, and he acts like nothing happened. Wow, and all in the process of trying to get away from some random dude who was trying to pop game. OMG! Only you. Seriously, you know you're welcome at this house for as long as you need. I cleared it with my momma."

"Thank you. I need to thank your mother too. It seems like she has a full house, and I hate to put her out," she expressed.

"Honey child, please. She loves a full house. Besides, Khan will be leaving soon. He hasn't spent the night since he and Nehemiah graduated from West Virginia University. You know my brother got his own place. He just stays here when Daddy is gone on long hauls."

"You're sure?"

"Yes, now come on, it's prayer time. The only way to have a breakthrough is to take it to the Lord in prayer. Let me get Momma, you know she's a prayer warrior. God is going to make it better," she preached.

That was true. Royale knew all that in her heart, but she had a lot blocking her passage to God. Her prayer life had grown cold. She did what was expected during her mission, but her personal relationship with God was just as disconnected as her relationship with her family. It felt like at times, she wanted to hold on to her anger more than she wanted to let go of it because after the anger subsided, she'd have to deal with the real issues, the ones she kept running from. That wasn't healthy, but it was how she was surviving.

"Come on, Royale, Momma is waiting for us," Kisha called.

Royale got up from the table, the day had worn her out. She knew her cousin was worried because by now, the internet had to be lit with her personal business. She had yet to answer her phone, and she needed to at least talk to Rina, and she would. After praying, she would call her.

CHAPTER 4

"Where are you going, boy?" Ronald asked his son.

"Work, Pop."

"You got all that education, doubled majored in landscape architecture and horticulture and all you do is cut grass."

"No, it's not all I do. It's all you think I do," he corrected. His father had no idea of his accomplishments. He had a contract with the county and had offers from other states. In fact, they didn't have to even live in a trailer park. He could afford a mini-mansion in the suburbs, but his father was content, so he let it be.

"If you told me, then I'd know. Why have you been coming in late at night? Did you get a girlfriend? I hope it's that Everleigh Jacobs. That's a woman."

Khan rolled his eyes but had his back turned to his father, so he didn't see it. Ronald liked Everleigh because she held the same ignorant ideology as him, which Khan found out later. All about preserving the white race and keeping the bloodline pure, as if a race of people were thoroughbred horses. Honestly, he was too educated to be attracted to that kind of woman. He went out on a few dates with her and he was done.

"Pop, I'm heading out. I made you some lunch. If I'm late getting back, Ms. Shirley said she'd bring you over supper. Oh, and I fixed your truck, so you should be good. Do you need anything else before I go?"

"Well, when you come back, get me some more beer. I'm down to six cans."

Khan nodded, though he knew his father didn't need it. The man probably urinated beer, knowing the doctors had warned him about his alcohol intake, as well as his habit of taking his medication with his beer. The only time he wasn't drinking was when he had to do work for the Klan he was associated with.

Saying goodbye, Khan quickly exited the home and headed to his work truck. He was on his way to Momma Byse's house to redo her landscaping, mow her lawn and check out her greenhouse. He never charged her, seeing as how she kept him fed all throughout high school and college, basically becoming the maternal figure he needed and his saving grace. It was her guidance that kept him from becoming a racist like his father.

An hour and a half later, Khan arrived at the Byse's home. He would've arrived earlier, but he had gotten a call from one of the supervisors that worked for him. Once he handled their issue, he headed to his best customer.

Khan got out of his truck and started to remove his tools and machinery. Once that was done, he sauntered around the exterior of the yard to see where and what he wanted to do first. He was humming a little tune to himself when he spotted Royale. She was busy as a bee, digging. She wore blue jean cutoffs, a fitted T-shirt, and had her earbuds in her ear. As he approached her, he heard her rapping. She was definitely into it because he stood there a good three minutes before she noticed his presence.

"Sorry. Mrs. Byse said you were coming over. She and Kisha are at the prison doing their ministry and Nehemiah's at work. I told Mrs. Byse I would assist you if you needed. I just got caught up in tending to her flowers," she told him while taking out her earbuds, but she was still in a sitting position. He couldn't help but smile at her. She really was a beautiful girl, and those deep Gabrielle Union dimples bewitched him. He could stare at her all day long and never grow tired. He must have been looking too hard because she dropped her head slightly, and he could see crimson coloring her neck.

"No apologies needed. I think I can put you to work, but what are you listening to?" he asked, extending his hand to assist her with getting up off the ground.

"That was NF's song 'I'll Keep On'. It's part of my quiet time."

He wasn't much of a religious man and wasn't sure what quiet time was. He did attend church at the urging of Momma Byse, but he wasn't dedicated like she was. Khan had never been baptized. Attending church with the Byse family was difficult to keep from his dad. The church he attended was diverse, but his father didn't believe in mixing in that way. Royale must have noticed his confusion, so she explained.

"Quiet time is my personal time with God. I usually read some scriptures, let them marinate, pray, and then write in my journal. Today, I just needed that extra boost, and I love music."

"Is that so? What kind of music do you like?" he asked, intrigued. His tongue glided the circumference of his mouth. Khan kept his eyes locked with hers. She was mesmerizing without even trying. Who was this woman who he was completely taken by?

"I listen to everything. My grandmother is gospel great, Patty Royce, winner of numerous Dove awards, NAACP and BET awards. I listen to all kinds of gospel and Contemporary Christian music like, for King & Country, and Christian rap like KB and NF. Basically, I listen to a little bit of everything."

"Country?" he asked, impressed that her grandmother was *the* Patty Royce. Momma Byse wore that woman's music out, so even he knew a song or two by heart.

"Yes, I used to take clogging, so I know country music."

For some reason, that cracked him up, and he doubled over and laughed. He didn't take her for a clog dancer.

"It's not that funny."

"I'm sorry, but I just visualized you clogging on the *Hee Haw* show."

"*Ha-ha*. Anyway, do you need something to eat? I made some cinnamon honey drop biscuits."

Khan stopped laughing as soon as he heard eat. He was definitely the kind of man who was impressed by good food. If she could cook like he thought she could, then he was about to fall head over meal in love. "I can't say I've ever had them kind of biscuits."

"Come try one, and then you can get to work," she instructed.

Not one to argue, Khan nodded and followed her into the house. It really surprised him how friendly and open she was with him, considering he was a stranger to her and her life story was all over television. It also shocked him how easily they fell into conversation.

As soon as he entered the kitchen, the smell of cinnamon and honey serenaded his nostrils and his stomach growled in approval. Breakfast had been the last meal he consumed and he needed a snack. A man of his size was always hungry. He washed his hands, then sat at the table and watched as Royale put two biscuits on the plate for him, and one for herself. He was impressed by her thoughtfulness.

"Would you like a dollop of honey? I always dip my biscuits in honey."

Cute. Royale was just sweet. A smile quickly lit his face at how genuinely excited she was, so he agreed to the honey. Then she placed the plate in front of him and set her plate down before taking the chair beside him. His mouth was watering just at the scent alone.

Khan lifted his large hand to pick up the biscuit but was intercepted by Royale's much smaller, feminine hand. She latched onto his hand and began to bless the food. So, he followed suit. After she said amen, they both began to eat. Lord have mercy, that was some good eating. He finished his two biscuits before she started on her one, then got himself two more. While they ate, they chatted.

"Kisha was right about you."

"How so?" he queried, watching her as her tongue wiped away the honey tarrying on her bottom lip. He readjusted himself and tried to refocus his thoughts. The woman had a way of distracting him.

"She suggested that you were easy to get along with and that I'd feel comfortable in your presence."

He grinned. He would have to remember to thank Kisha later. "I was just thinking the same about you." Royale offered him a sheepish grin, unable to hide her blush. It was cute to see her amber skin glow red. Whoever said you couldn't see a blush on a black woman hadn't met Royale. It was becoming his favorite thing to witness.

There was a brief pause before she spoke again. Khan was ogling her, while her attention was on her plate. "Thank you, Khan."

"Um, for what exactly?" he asked as he licked his fingers clean, cutting his eyes away from her as she glanced at him. He wanted to thank her for the delicious biscuits. Yeah, he had a new favorite dish and a new crush. A dangerous crush because if his father found out… But right now, he didn't care about what anyone else thought. Royale was special. He knew that after meeting her.

"Thank you for not asking about my face, not making a fuss about who my family is, and overall, not prying. It was really nice to talk to someone and not feel judged or pitied."

He took his time before replying. He could tell that even behind the pretty grin, she was hurting and most likely felt like no one understood her. Kind of like he felt when his mother was murdered and instead of his dad getting him help, he tried to teach him to hate. "Honestly, last night when I helped you, I wanted to ask you what happened. I thought you were running from an abusive boyfriend or something. Your SUV was packed full, and you seemed so terrified."

"Not quite an abusive boyfriend, but I assume you're aware of the ignominy surrounding my family. When I arrived home, my sissy or her mom was supposed to pick me up, but somehow, my dad convinced them that he'd come get me. Long story short, we had a mini-blowup at the airport that led to him slapping me."

Khan shook his head in anger. He knew all about dads who hit their children. The idea of a man, any man, putting hands on Royale made him livid. He would not stand by and allow it to continue. "Is he after you? Do you need protection?" He was a hunter with a crack shot. As a matter of fact, he had a gun in his work truck that was locked and loaded. "I always carry, if you get my drift, and I never miss."

Royale's honey copper eyes darkened and widened at his offer. "Oh no, it's not that serious. Dad was just upset. He has never raised a hand to me before. I didn't leave because of that, really. I left because I felt like I was suffocating. I'm not ready to deal with the pain. It's overbearing sometimes." She shook her head as if she didn't mean to reveal that. "I'm sorry, Khan. You came here to do a job, not listen to a stranger complaining. It's just that you're such a good listener, and so easy to talk with. I just feel like I've known you for years and not just a day."

"Hold up," he interrupted, putting up his hands to stop her, "don't apologize. True enough, we only met last night, but any friend of the Byse family is a friend of mine. How about you help me with the yard work so I can burn off these carbs after eating four of your delicious biscuits, and we can talk. It can be about anything. You have my word I'll not repeat what you say to another soul. I cross my heart, hope to die, and stick a needle in my eye," he told her and winked.

Royale giggled, showcasing her dimples, and that made him smile also. The sound she made was heavenly. He could see himself falling hard for her. Crazy how he wasn't looking for a woman, and God had just sent him an angel. Whether she knew it or not, she totally had him and he was awestruck at the power she willed on him so quickly.

"Same here, Khan."

♦ ♦ ♦

Grayling had just left a meeting with his attorney, his publicist, personal assistant and the church board. It had been that kind of day. Thanks to Matan, the whole situation was at the forefront of the news and the internet again. His team attempted to take down the offending videos that had been recorded at Starbucks, but there were so many, it didn't really matter. The point was, this didn't look good for the church. It was a huge distraction that he needed to get a handle on, but in the age of technology, nothing could be totally erased.

Grayling really hated how this was impacting the church family and his family. One decision made by two people had turned his and Royale's world upside down. He was doing his best to rebuild his flocks' faith and trust in him, and he was making headway until now. It was starting all over again.

When he entered his office, he picked up the Aleve pills and the Evian water bottle that his sister had left for him. After taking the medicine, he flopped down in his office chair, clasped his hands and started to pray.

Our Father in heaven, hallowed be thy name. Father, I come to You with a humble heart and troubled mind. I have sinned by hurting my daughter, and we need You now, Lord. Guide my actions and help me to be an imitation of Your Son and not this world. Please protect my family and the church members through this tough time. I'm weakening, Lord, and I don't want to fail them in any way. I've allowed this situation with my wife to separate me from You, my daughter, and my flock. I can't be useful if I'm distracted. Help me overcome this moment and rise above the negative and just be in You. In Jesus' Name, I ask, Amen.

Just as he ended his prayer, his secretary buzzed him to let him know that Roslyn was on line two. His first thought was to tell Betsy Mae to take a message, but if he did that, Roslyn would only hound her, and Betsy Mae was sixty-five and didn't need to deal with that aggravation. Roslyn had been a great member of the church, and an extension of the family until two months ago when everyone found out about the affair her son was having with his wife. Taking a deep breath to mentally prepare himself, he picked up the phone and answered.

"Bishop Chastain?"

"Yes, Sister Roslyn, it's me. How can I assist you today?" he asked, hoping the sound of discontent and annoyance couldn't be read in his tone. God forgive him, but he just didn't want to be bothered with whatever drama she was offering.

"Well, I know you've seen this madness. The media is just slandering my poor son's name, and all he was doing was attempting to talk to Roycee," she stated panickily. He was about to respond, but she interrupted. "This has taken a toll on my baby. He's so stressed out, and you know this won't bode well for his future. He wants to attend Boston University School of Theology, but if the media doesn't stop their attacks on him, he may never see his dream come to fruition. Can't you do something?"

Grayling took his left hand and rubbed the side of his head. Yes, he was a man of God, but he was still a man. What did she want him to do? Prior to him finding out about the affair, he had assisted Matan in choosing schools and had written him letters of recommendations. It was Matan who chose to not return to his current graduate program, which was a slap in Grayling's face. He worked hard to assist Matan.

Now, she wanted him to do more for her son who'd had an affair with his wife. A son he had mentored, counseled and treated like a son well up until he found out about his traitorous deed. The only person he was concerned about was his daughter. "Sister Roslyn, what exactly do you want me to do? I have no control over the media. I didn't tell your son to approach my daughter. Matan is no longer a child; he is a grown man and has to deal with the consequences of his actions." As soon as he heard her gasp, he knew it was about to be something. She was all for the dramatics, and she got off on being extra. He closed his eyes and asked God for patience.

"Well, I never. So, you're blaming my son, when your wife, who is twice his age, seduced him. You know how my son looks up to you, being that he's never had a father. I mean, if things had worked out like they should have, you would've been his father anyway. I can't believe you're turning your back on us like his no-good, incarcerated father. So, instead of forgiving him, you're judging him and refusing to help him. You're our pastor, the leader of the flock. He strayed, yes, but doesn't Matthew 18:12 say, *What do you think? If a man owns a hundred sheep, and one of them wanders away, will he not leave the ninety-nine on the hills and go to look for the one that wandered off?* I want you to fix it! You know enough people."

Grayling rolled his eyes. The father he had, wasn't as bad as Roslyn wanted people to believe. Matan's father's only fault was that he really loved Roslyn.

Grayling grew tired of Sister Roslyn always saying he should have been Matan's father, all because, back in the day they dated. However, he was not about to play Bible verse war with her. "I've just got out of a meeting, and I'm doing the best I can to have the video pulled. I don't know what else you want me to do. I can't undo the past. I can only move forward, and honestly, right now, my greatest concern is my daughter. If you need prayer or counseling, I think it best one of the others on the team assist you. I'm going to be taking a leave of absence."

"What?"

Grayling started to repeat himself when he heard the dial tone. He hung the phone up and decided to call it a day. He needed to visit Royce anyway, and there was no reason why his leave of absence couldn't start right now. After giving Betsy Mae a few orders, he left and headed to the rehab his wife was in. She'd phoned earlier and told him they needed to talk, and he hoped it went better than his conversation with Roslyn.

*   *   *

After Khan left, Royale called Rina and gave her an update. It was so good to converse to someone who didn't want to take from her and who wasn't trying to get over on her. He just let her talk about things she was passionate about. It was a relief.

"Is he cute, though? That's all I need to know."

Royale sat on the bed with her legs crossed, grinning from ear to ear. "Yes, ma'am, and he's super sweet. He literally is just a big old teddy bear. He's built nicely too. I'm talking, muscles on top of muscles, and he's so tall. Girl, he loves my cinnamon honey drop biscuits. He told me he knew I could cook."

"How?"

"Because you know I'm cornbread with a side of gravy thick." Royale giggled while thinking about how much fun she had spending time with Khan. He was really good at his job too. She couldn't believe a good catch like him wasn't already married.

"Not anymore. You're more like half a cup of brown rice and a side salad without ranch dressing thin. Momma said to me last night that she hoped you aren't developing an eating disorder because ain't no man worth missing a meal over."

Royale threw her head back, laughing at Rina mimicking Gwendolyn. "That's the truth. Mrs. Byse is going to have me back at my ready weight with all the good food she cooks."

"Good. All joking aside, how are you? I was so worried after that Starbucks incident, and then your tire, girl, baby sister was coming to hunt you down."

"Today was so good. I laughed and had a great conversation. My quiet time was just right. I've been listening to NF's *Mansion* album. I feel ready to run the world."

"Okay, Beyoncé. That's good to hear."

Thinking about Beyoncé made her remember January, who was a big fan of the singer. "How is January doing? I feel so bad not doing my mentor duty."

"I talked to her, and she understands. She's doing really well, and she knows she can come to me as well."

"Wonderful, that's one less person I need to worry about."

"What else is bothering you? I can hear you chewing on your bottom lip."

For her and Rina to be first cousins, they were connected like twins. It was crazy how well they were mentally intertwined. "I have a confession."

"What?"

"I had an anxiety attack last night while I was driving, and I must have hit something, which caused the tire to blow. Like, I was hearing them talk about me on the radio, and I must have blacked out for a moment or something."

"Oh, my gosh. You didn't tell me that last night. That's dangerous, and you could've been seriously hurt. When did the anxiety attacks start?"

"When I was in Nairobi. I just developed them. I think I can get over it. It's just that I was stressed, worried, and scared, but I was keeping it all in."

"Let's pray, sissy. That is nothing to play with."

"You're right. Let's pray."

CHAPTER 5

Royce watched with falcon eyes as her husband sauntered into the facility, she'd been in for nearly two months. He looked different.

Grayling Chastain was always a handsome man, but now he was leaner and more built. He was reminiscent of the man she had met years ago. Her husband was fine, extremely so. His attractiveness matched with his drive and intellect, had her hooked on him from the moment they were introduced. Something was alluring about his deep chestnut skin and soft brown eyes. Grayling always had a smile on his face, with those deep dimples she loved to kiss until she betrayed his trust. Still, they were working on forgiving each other and moving forward.

"Hello, Bishop Chastain. I'm Janice Harper, your wife's counselor. I'm just here for emotional support for you both, as well as to make sure the conversation stays on track. Do you have any questions for me?"

"No," he replied bluntly.

"Okay. You two start whenever you are ready," Janice told them, sitting back down.

Watching her husband turn his dark eyes on her made her self-conscious. She didn't have on her armor. There was no makeup, false eyelashes or drawn in eyebrows. She was showing her bare skin, and in her mind, it wasn't as beautiful as it was in her youth. Royce wondered if he noticed.

Royce's lustrous natural hair was styled in a simple bun. Unfortunately, the facility wouldn't allow her to have her glam squad. That made her that much more nervous to see her husband. The last time they had spoken, he was angry. She thought he would topple her petite five feet frame. Shaking the thought, her eyes lingered on his, and she finally spoke. "Hello, Gray." She purposely used the intimate pet name to connect to what they used to be. Royce knew her actions had deeply hurt him, and she didn't want their marriage to end.

"Ro," he replied coolly before taking his seat adjacent to her.

"We're missing one. Where's Roycee? I thought she was supposed to be back in town now."

He sighed. "Well, about that. She's not coming because she isn't ready to speak to you, or me for that matter. Also, she had a run-in with Matan that's all-over social media and it has brought the incident back up."

That made her ears perk up. Royce hadn't spoken to Matan, though she needed to do so. "She's still upset. I thought after all this time away, she would have gotten to a better place. I mean, I'm her mother." As soon as the words left her mouth, she noticed how her husband tensed and his jaw went taut. Apparently, he didn't agree. "What?"

"Did you just hear what you said? There's not a limit to how long a person grieves a heartbreak. That was a loss for her. You and Matan broke her heart. Besides, she doesn't owe you anything. You betrayed your family, your vows, and God."

"Well then! Tell me how you really feel." Her voice elevated at his accusations.

"How long?"

The quick shift in conversation and the attitude that followed caused her to quiet. She was unprepared for his request, which left her at a loss as to how to reply to him. "What?"

"How *long* did you and Matan cheat? Aren't I here for you to finally confess all your sins? Tell me," he demanded, looking from her to the counselor.

Royce didn't want to get into that now. He wouldn't like the answer. Never in her life had she regretted anything she had done because each move she made was to get her to the next level. Her actions were to fulfill her needs and wants but seeing this side of Grayling had her thinking she had made the wrong move on the chess board.

"Royce, do you need a break?" Janice asked.

She shook her head no.

"How long, Ro?"

"One year," she whispered, but from the deep intake of breath he took, she knew he'd heard her loud and clear.

Silence lingered uncomfortably for a good five minutes after her confession. Then Grayling mumbled something inaudible before responding out loud. "A whole year isn't an affair, it's a relationship. I was mentoring him while the two of you were having sex all over Washington DC and Virginia. My goodness, the laughs you two must have had at mine and our daughter's expense. Royale was dreaming about marriage, and you were... I just don't believe this. Was he the only one?" he shot back.

Royce shook her head and rolled her eyes back, knowing she had to tell it all. "No." Grayling winced at her confession, and she could see the distress on his face. She didn't want to tell him that truth, but he needed to know, just in case her past came back to haunt her.

"No?" he queried, his head snapping up, and dark eyes clashing into her sable eyes. "What do you mean, no?"

Before she could answer, Janice intervened with concern in her voice. "Bishop Chastain, do you need a moment?"

"No, ma'am. I just need my wife to be honest. Apparently, our vows before God and family meant nothing to her. I was under the impression a marriage was between one man and one woman, but it seems my wife is under the impression we have an open marriage. I'm waiting, Royce," he retorted calmly.

"I...see... Well, since I've been here, I've learned some things. Honestly, I never heard the term 'emotional affair'—she used air quotes— "but the other men weren't physical. I didn't have sex with them. I leaned on them for emotional support." She watched as an array of emotions danced across his handsome face. "I'm sorry."

"How long were these *emotional affairs*, how many men, and why?" he interrogated.

Royce couldn't read his face. His voice was even toned and calm; there was no inflection in his voice or aggression in his body language. She grew nervous thinking that he was shutting down. He just might flip on her when she answered his questions. He wasn't going to be happy. "It all started ten years ago, right when you were becoming popular on television and had all those speaking engagements. You were busy and didn't have time for Roycee or me—"

"Don't call her that. Royale now hates the name Roycee," he interrupted, clearly disturbed and perturbed by her admission.

"Oh, okay. Can I continue?" she queried in a submissive manner.

Grayling acknowledged her request nonverbally by nodding, as his lips remained sealed like a Ziploc bag, which had her rethinking answering the questions he'd asked. Taking a deep sigh and calming her shook nerves, she continued.

"Well, it was when you were getting really busy, and I met a man, not in the church, just a friend. Sometimes we'd go out when you forgot about me. You forgot our anniversary, my birthday, and I didn't feel loved or cared for. I was no longer your helpmate. I felt like your doormat. For approximately ten years, I had emotional affairs with five different men before I had a sexual affair with Matan."

Grayling continued nodding his head but remained silent. She wasn't sure if that was a good thing or not. She'd rather know what he was thinking than have him be quiet and say nothing.

"Bishop Chastain, can you express to your wife how her admission makes you feel?" Janice urged to get the conversation flowing again.

"I feel like crap. I feel like I've been suckered because apparently, I have no idea who I married. You've been with other men. You've been out on dates, and then with your daughter's soon-to-be fiancé, and somehow that's my fault. You're basically saying you cheated, emotionally and sexually, because I was doing what God called me to do." He started moving his hands to further describe his dismay with the situation, but he continued speaking, his eyes dead centered on his wife. "What I fail to comprehend is how did I ever make you a doormat? You? As if you would ever allow that. Plus, I've never walked over you or tried to control your overly grown, spoiled behind. That might have been the problem." He paused, shaking his head and collecting his thought. "Really! Not one time did you ask me to slow down because you were too busy reaping the benefits. Right? You wanted the prestige, power, and respect of being the first lady, but you didn't want the hard work or the sacrifice. Typical Royce, always putting the blame on someone else. You did what you wanted to do."

Royce did her best not to flinch at his allegation and characterization of her. She thought he was harsh in his illustration of her personality. By no means was she innocent, but she wasn't fully to blame either. She, Grayling and Matan all shared some fault, but now wasn't the time to point that out. "I was lonely, Gray."

"No, you were selfish, Ro. If it were only the emotional affairs, I could get over that. However, the fact that you were in bed with another man—not just any man, but one who our daughter loved, one I mentored and treated like a son—that cuts deeply. I don't know if the wound will ever heal."

"I love you, Gray. I made a mistake."

"*A mistake*? No, a mistake was the first emotional affair. What you did was make conscious decisions several times to sin and be unfaithful to your faithful husband. What you did was choose your wants over your own family's needs. You let your carnal mind lead. My goodness, Ro, the boy was just twenty-three. You knew better, even if he didn't. You being unfaithful isn't my fault at all. It's on you." Shaking his head in disgust, he continued, his voice less harsh, but still full of emotion. "We counsel couples together about this very thing, and you were swimming in sin. So selfish. Your actions didn't just affect you, they affected lots of other innocent people and for what, pleasure and attention? Was it worth it?"

"Of course, it wasn't worth it. Gray forgive me, please," she pleaded. Royce knew he would be in his feelings, but all this extra was worrying her last nerve. She hated when he got preachy.

"It won't happen overnight. I pray I can forgive you. I mean, I will, but I'll never forget this. I can't. It won't be easy, but I won't lose my daughter to gain my wife."

Royce wasn't sure what to make of his latter statement, but she nodded anyway. He was upset and emotional, but at least he was willing to forgive her. The tension in her body slowly dissipated, and she felt like they were on the right track now. She just had to get Gray back in the palm of her hand again.

"If that's all, I guess I should go. I need to see if Rina has heard from Royale."

"Where is she?"

"I don't know for sure; I just know she left the state and will only talk to Rina."

"What? She's not talking to my momma, daddy or even Gwendolyn?"

"Nope."

"I'm sure my daddy can find her, but in the meantime, I'll pray for her," she offered, wondering why her daughter was avoiding home. It wasn't like Royale had to deal with her. Part of her understood her daughter's pain and embarrassment, but to run this long was just a bit much. At the end of the day, they were family, and if Gray, her husband, could come see her, then certainly, Royale could do the same.

He gave a heartless chuckle before responding, "Pray for yourself too. Bye, Ro."

"Bye, Gray." She watched him go, unsure of the state of their marriage, but willing to do what was necessary to keep it intact. Even though she'd been having an affair, she wanted her husband.

"Royce, you didn't tell him what we discussed," Janice reminded her.

Royce sighed before dropping her head into her hands. "I couldn't, Janice. I've put too much on him as is. I'll tell him next week. I promise. I have another month here. Besides, you heard him, our daughter is having a tough time."

◆ ◆ ◆

Tears fell down Grayling's eyes as he drove away from the rehab facility. He couldn't believe Royce had been lying to him for ten years. *Ten years!* Had he really been that caught up in his ministry that he didn't notice his wife's infidelity? How could he marry a total stranger? He didn't know the woman at all. Every part of him wanted to find every man she had shared intimate thoughts, time and her body with and end their existence. Lord knows he wasn't always saved. He was born a sinner like everyone else. He didn't come from wealth or connections, but he had made a promise to his parents he would only follow where God led. But right now, at this moment, he wanted to react in a worldly manner. So much of him wanted to act out and do to his wife what she had done to him.

It hurt him severely that Royce could speak so casually about her infidelities. He grabbed his head to calm the pounding. Another headache was brewing, and they were becoming as common as breathing. If he didn't get a hold of things, he would have a stroke and a heart attack, and it wasn't worth it. However, he was so tired. The session he had with his wife had been more draining than he'd anticipated. Shaking the conversation, he started up his truck and drove off with a million and one thoughts antagonizing his mind.

Somehow, he ended up at a bar. He wasn't really a drinker, but tonight, he needed some bourbon to numb the mess Royce had made, and he didn't want to drink alone. So, he phoned his closest friend, and godfather to his daughter, Antwon.

Antwon was a person he trusted with everything. They had grown up together like brothers, and Ant always kept it real. Right now, that was exactly what he needed.

"G, you okay?" Antwon's deep tenor voice asked as they gave each other a man hug and entered the bar. Antwon was taller than Grayling at 6'2", but they had the same width. It was Antwon who had gotten Grayling back in the gym to buff him up. In contrast to Grayling's molasses coloring, his friend had a light cinnamon color, due to his mother being American Indian.

"Ant, man, I went to talk to Ro and, bruh, she told me she's been having affairs on the regular for the past ten years. She claims for nine years, she's had emotional affairs, and the affair with Matan lasted a year. Then she's claiming she was alone and that's why it happened. Like, she is blaming me for working, for doing God's work. That's why she sought other men."

"Whoa, what?"

"Yeah, and now I wonder if Royale hadn't caught them in the act, would they still be continuing their affair. I mean, what was their endgame? I didn't ask that because I was too far gone with all the information, she had disclosed. Now I have to find out where Royale is."

"I saw the Starbucks video. I was hot that ole boy was coming at her like that. Is she okay? I know when I called you, I couldn't get you. I thought you had hemmed Matan up."

Grayling sighed and looked at his friend. "I hit her, Antwon. I slapped my daughter because she told the truth and I just reacted. She looked at me like her entire world had ended. When I went to Gwen's house to see her, she avoided me. I just feel sick and stuck. My wife cheats, my daughter runs, and I'm falling apart."

"G, you didn't," he whispered, looking confused and concerned.

Grayling shook his head in shame. He regretted it. "I did. I'm also taking a leave of absence from the church. I need to get my family in order. I got to get Royale back."

"Yeah, but before that, you need a drink, my friend. Then we'll come up with a plan to get my goddaughter back here and handle Matan. He betta never come at Royale like that again! Please believe I'm an old-school hoodlum. You know I only let him go unscathed based on the strength of you, but I'll get amnesia in a minute when it comes to Royale."

Grayling just nodded his head.

◆ ◆ ◆

The next morning, Grayling was awakened by his cellphone ringing. He ignored it, and a few minutes later, the house phone sounded off. He knew it had to be important because, after the fallout of his wife's infidelity, he had changed all the phone numbers associated with him except the one at the church.

"Hello?" he managed to mumble. He was struggling to open his sleep-filled eyes. He and Antwon ended up talking more than anything. He needed a new perspective.

"Bishop Chastain, good morning, it's Marc Perkins. I just wanted to touch base with you about the reality show."

"Huh?" That statement woke him all the way up, causing him to throw off the down comforter. Ever since his wife had gone to rehab, he'd been sleeping in the guest room that was set up like a hotel room. He feared his wife may have taken her lover in their bed, and he couldn't handle that. He had yet to ask her, but that was one of those things better left unknown. He had already ordered a new bed and mattress. The sound of Marc's nasal, high-pitched voice drew him out of his mental thoughts.

"Well, since Royce is in rehab, I was thinking, why not do a spin-off and give Royce her own show. She loves the idea. The concept would be us following you both around as you rebuild your marriage. The fans want to know what's going on. We all love a happy ending."

Grayling pulled the phone from his ear and looked at it as if Marc could read his facial expression. It seemed Marc was on that same dumbness his wife was on. "Absolutely not!"

"Okay, I see you need to think about the idea. How about Royale? Can you get her to come back to the show? The fans want to know about her. How is she handling what happened between her mother and boyfriend? She's been silent, out of the media, and the world is hungry to know how she feels. Heck, I can get her, her own reality show. That Starbucks video was everything, and it lit up Black Twitter. Well, actually, it just lit up Twitter. She was trending and doesn't even have an account, even Fetty Wap got into it."

"Fetty who?"

Marc sucked his teeth. "He's a secular rapper. Apparently, when the men were arguing, they were quoting his lyrics. We can really make lots of money on this. The world needs a good girl. Mothers love Royale as a role model for their daughters. If we can get her name attached to Olivia Hoover, who, by the way, is blowing up with her memoir, that would be epic. They're acquainted, right? Christian girls are the new *it* thing."

Now Grayling was extremely annoyed. Olivia's maternal grandparents were members of his church, but he didn't know how Marc had found that out. His daughter was not a dividend or a media entity. He wasn't going to exploit his daughter's embarrassment and pain. Everything didn't need to be made public, and Marc should understand that. "Marc, the answer is no. My family is broken. I won't put my daughter or myself in the public spotlight anymore. Not happening, ever. I can't speak for Royce, but my daughter and I *will not* participate in any more reality shows. We. Are. Done."

"What about Rina? I can work that angle too. Her story is powerful."

Grayling hung up and dropped his head back on the pillow and shut his eyes. He was tired, both physically and mentally, and had been since the scandal broke. This was too much. Why would Royce even think about being back on a stupid show? A part of him wanted to call

Royce to find out exactly how much of the idea was Marc and how much was her. What was she thinking? The last thing they needed were cameras in their life.

Getting up out of bed, he reached over to the nightstand and lifted his Bible and opened it to the New Testament where he read 1 John 5:5-13. After reading the scriptures, he dropped his head and prayed for his family, church family and himself. He asked God to give him strength during this season in his life. He asked for guidance and strength as the fiery darts came left and right. He knew what he needed was the armor of God and a shield of faith. It was starting, but this time, he was going to be prepared.

CHAPTER 6

Khan pulled out the letter he had from Kalid Giles, the man convicted of his mother's murder. He requested that Khan come visit him and explained that he had put Khan on the list so he could come whenever he was comfortable.

Dear Khan,

I'm not sure how to start this letter because I fear whatever I write will offend you. That's something I never want to do. It's been a long time. The last time we saw each other, you were about to turn ten. It's been about fifteen years. That's a long time not to know the truth about what happened to your mother. I swear to you, son, I didn't murder Khloe. I could never do that. I would like for you to come and see me. I've added your name to my list of visitors. I completely understand if you aren't ready now, but know that the offer has no time limit. I want you to know the truth, not the lies the prosecutor spewed in the courtroom. The Innocence Project has taken on my case and will prove without a shadow of a doubt that I'm innocent.

I'm so very sorry your mother was taken from you. That breaks my heart in ways you will never know. I do know your mother would be so proud of your accomplishments. It takes a courageous young man to overcome the tragedy and heartbreak you've suffered. Hopefully, you and I will be able to talk soon.

-Kalid

When he first read the letter, he was angry, but the more he read it, the more questions he had. Those questions were behind the excursion to Mount Olive Correctional Complex, a maximum-security prison that held the man accused of murdering his mother. It wasn't the first time he had driven past this facility; it was less than an hour's drive from him. He knew where Kalid was but had never had the strength to face him. He couldn't visit today anyway because visitation days were Saturdays and Sundays. He had familiarized himself with the visitation brochure, so he knew what to expect. This coming weekend he planned to come back and visit. Turning his truck back on, he headed back towards Charleston, but he wasn't going home, he was going to his mother's gravesite.

♦ ♦ ♦

When Khan arrived home later that evening, he knew it was going to be one of those nights. Some of his dad's friends, including his old cop buddies, were hanging outside. For some reason, the letter he had on him felt like it was scorching his skin. If his father ever found out, it would be the end of his existence. It sounded like things were getting rowdy, and it didn't take long for him to find out what had his dad in such a state.

"Khan, where you been, boy?" Ronald asked, eyes red from drinking. Khan knew he was in his element, hanging out with men who held his philosophy. *Here they go.* Every time he came home, his father always asked him where he'd been. "Pop, I do work. Being the owner of the business means I'm the last to leave. What's wrong?" he inquired as he greeted the other men with nods and handshakes.

"The legal system sucks. They're granting that murderer, the man who killed your sweet momma, a new trial. Apparently, there is some new evidence and DNA. I mean, there are allegations that the crime lab mishandled evidence and that there was prosecutorial misconduct."

"Don't make no sense. We need to do something about it," Hoss instigated.

Khan looked over at the overweight man who was barely 5'8". He was covered in tattoos, had a receding hairline, and his hair was completely white-gray. The most distinctive feature about him was his rosacea-stained cheeks. He looked like a country Santa Claus.

"Yeah, you right, Hoss. Ain't none of this mess started until they reelected that black president and then started shouting *Black Lives Matter*. Well, white ones do too. My wife would still be alive if not for Kalid," Ronald fumed.

Khan remained mummed as his mind went back to the letter, he'd received from Kalid. He had no idea Kalid was getting a new trial. That was an interesting development. He wondered how long he had been holding onto that information. Why hadn't it been in the news?

"Khan, did you hear me?"

"Yeah, Pop, I heard you. I'm just flabbergasted by the information. It's been nearly two decades, and now it's all about to be back in the media again. It's a lot to deal with at once."

"Yeah, well, you need to testify this time. You was too young last time, but the jury needs to hear from you. Tell them how you saw him kill your mother. Freaking animal. I mean, he's an animal to kill my wife, but then to do it in front of my son. I shoulda killed him."

Too young? He was too damaged. His father had made him attend the trial when he should have been on a therapist's couch, getting help. He wouldn't be a good witness because whatever he knew from the murder was his father's recollection of it. He had yet to put the flashbacks he was having in the correct sequence. For fifteen years, he did his best to un-see it all. Add the trauma of the verbal and physical abuse he faced from his father and his mind was all jumbled. "I don't remember it. It's like my mind refuses to open that door," he explained. The entire group of men grew silent as if they sympathized with him. Well, everyone except his father.

"You better remember, or you're going to let a guilty man get off to kill another innocent white woman. What good are you? He should've killed you too."

There it was. It wasn't the first time his father had made that statement, and it wouldn't be the last.

"Be easy on him, Ronald. I'm sure when the time comes, he'll come through," Hoss added.

Khan wasn't fazed by his father's crass and careless statement. He really was over the conversation. He wanted to see Royale. She and Kisha had invited him to go with them to a movie, and he really needed something to get his mind off everything that was currently happening.

"Excuse me. I got to shower and then head back out. Y'all make sure he doesn't drink too much."

"Whatever! Hey, where you going? All this week, you been gone more than you've been home."

There was no way he was telling Ronald where he was going. He didn't need to start an argument. It would probably go too far, and he wasn't letting anybody hurt the Byse family or Royale. "I have a social life." That was all he said before excusing himself and getting right back into the truck he had exited out of.

♦ ♦ ♦

Ronald watched his son leave and shook his head. He felt like he was losing his son. Maybe if he had told his son the reason, he was drunk at the bar was because that was when he'd actually found out Kalid was getting a new trial, and even though he was pushing for his son to testify, he also feared the truth coming out. Khloe was pregnant, but he had pulled some strings in order to keep that information hidden. If Khan found out, he might just lose him forever. Then again, he didn't even know Khan anymore. He rejected the lifestyle Ronald had embedded himself in ever since the murder of his wife.

"Ronald, you okay?" Hoss asked.

"I'm losing. That boy acts more like my sister every day. It's like he don't care that them coloreds took my wife and his mother from us. We got to build an army to defeat them devils, and he's all about embracing unity and crap. I swear, if I find out he's still going over to that Byse woman's house, I'm going to reign terror on him and that woman. I told her to mind her own business."

"That's their problem, they got them Civil Rights Amendments in the Constitution, then after that, they thought they were equal to a white man. Now that they reelected that Muslim, they think they can do anything. All of 'em need to be put in their place. If we want to win the war, we gotta step up and out the hoods. We need power suits and tattoo-free mouthpieces, and that'll bring in some new blood. Same terror, just a more professional look."

Ronald nodded his head in agreement. Hoss was right. He'd been forced to retire after he killed a young black man. It was all politics if you asked him. He was doing a routine stop when he smelled marijuana. There were a group of three men in the car, all acting suspicious. The passengers fled, leaving the driver, and he went in pursuit when he felt something hit him. He thought he had been shot, so he turned around and shot the driver, killing him.

"Ronald are you with us?" Winston asked.

"I am, I was just reminiscing."

"Well, we miss you on the beat."

"I miss it too."

"I gotta go. Y'all let me know what trouble we're getting into next week. I hear they're having a Black Lives Matter rally. I say we have a Blue Lives Matter rally, and then, later, show them why they ought to fear us."

Hoss laughed. "I hear you, brother. If Ronald wants, we can burn a few crosses in the Byse's yard. They need reminding. Let'em get too comfortable, they start thinking they own something. Better to get'em in line early. Besides, we owe that Byse family something. I know the husband stays gone on them long hauls, so, whenever you ready to start something."

Ronald and Winston laughed.

"That they do, they most certainly do," Ronald agreed. He was also thinking about connecting to his friends on the inside and having them permanently eliminate his problem, Kalid Giles. If the man was dead, he would no longer be a thorn in his side.

◆ ◆ ◆

Khan arrived at Momma Byse's house thirty minutes later. The women weren't quite ready, so he and Nehemiah talked, and he shared the letter with him, and about Kalid getting a new trial. Just as Nehemiah was about to reply, the women came downstairs giggling. Immediately, Khan's eyes went to Royale. She looked gorgeous. She wore only lip gloss. Her natural beauty was more than enough, as her skin was smooth and unblemished. Her honey eyes were carefree, and she looked relaxed. Though she'd been at the Byse's for less than a week, she seemed to be putting on weight. He liked that. She wore a royal purple fit and flare dress, and it fit her frame like a glove. She paired it with silver sparkling flats and white gold jewelry.

"Dang Khan how long are you going to stare at her?" Kisha teased.

Never one to be embarrassed, Khan just rolled with it. "For as long as she'll allow me." Then he turned his attention back to Royale, got up off the couch and approached her. "You look beautiful."

He watched as a blush dressed her exposed flesh, and she did her best to not catch his eyes. "Thank you."

"You're welcome. Shall we?"

"Khan, this isn't a date," Kisha warned.

Khan waved her off and looped Royale's arm in his. Tonight, may not be a date, but he was letting Royale know right now that he was interested in her, and he didn't care about the consequences.

♦ ♦ ♦

After the movie, they decided to go to The Chop House Charleston located in Charleston Town Center to eat. Khan was still in awe that the girls chose to watch Mission Impossible- Rogue Nation. More and more, he found himself liking Royale. He was attracted to her physical beauty, but he also liked that she didn't act Hollywood. She was a real woman, not at all stuck up or pretentious like her mother seemed to be on the reality show.

Originally, when he found out who she was, he thought it possible that she was putting on an act, but no, nothing was an act. Royale was a down to earth woman with a sweet personality. He noticed that she really was hurt by her mother's betrayal. He also liked that she wasn't a fake Christian. She did her quiet time every morning, and she helped Momma Byse doing the yard and housework. He admired and respected her for that. She was a different kind of woman, and it made him want to be in her presence so much more.

Pulling himself back into their current conversation, he opened the door for both women. Nehemiah was right behind him. The ladies told the host that they had a party of four. While they waited their turn, they all huddled together to talk about the movie. Khan was so into the conversation that he didn't notice an unwelcome guest arrive until she said his name.

"Khan, is that you?"

Khan's head popped up at the sound of the raspy voice. He mentally sighed. It was Heather, daughter of Hoss. She was heavy set and looked like her father. The only difference was she had white-blonde hair. Hopefully, this would go well. "Hey, Heather. How are you?" he queried as friendly as possible.

Khan observed her taking in his friends, and after a moment of silence, she spoke. "Um…so who are your *friends*? I don't think you've ever brought them around."

There was such distaste in her tone that Khan paused before speaking. He knew Heather was just as prejudiced and racist as her father. Before he could answer her, Everleigh appeared. She had dark ginger hair and deep green eyes. She was tall with a curvy figure. He was surprised to see Everleigh and Heather together since neither liked each other while he briefly dated Everleigh. The reason was, Heather had a crush on him, but he was dating Everleigh, and even though it didn't last long, it was long enough for Heather to get in her feels about it. He wondered why the two of them were together now.

"Khan, baby, it's been ages." Everleigh started acting way too familiar.

Khan noted the sour look on her face as well when she took in his guest. Everleigh knew Nehemiah, who never cared for her, but was always polite whenever they crossed paths, which was extremely limited.

"Byse, party of four?"

"C'mon, Khan, that's us," Nehemiah interrupted.

"Excuse me, ladies," Khan told them, then walked out, making sure he rested his hand on Royale's lower back and navigated her toward their awaiting booth. He could feel Heather and Everleigh's eyes on him, but he was unbothered. As they sat down, Nehemiah caught Khan's eye, and he nodded in silent communication. It was possible that more of his father's white supremacist friends were with Heather and Everleigh. If that were true, then the situation might turn dangerous, which had him rethinking that whole not caring about consequences. Neither of them wanted Kisha or Royale caught up in something that had nothing to do with them.

"Wasn't that your ex-girlfriend, Everleigh?" Kisha questioned.

"Not ex, but someone I previously dated." He left it at that as they began to look over the menu to see what they wanted. While doing that, they also had a little conversation.

No sooner than they ordered their drinks did Khan's cellphone began to ring. It was his father's ringtone. He excused himself and headed toward the men's bathroom to answer it.

"Yeah, Pop?"

"Are you coming home tonight?"

"I dunno."

"Well, I'm sorry about what I said, you know, about Kalid killing you too. That was the anger and alcohol talking. You know you're my only family. I was wrong to attack you like that."

Strange. Khan pulled the phone from his ear and looked at it as if he was looking at his father. The man had apologized. He never apologized. He was sure this conversation was going to be about his association with the enemy. "Okay, Pop. It's cool. Are you okay?"

"Yeah. I just pulled out the old photo albums, and I just got to thinking. We used to be happy. We used to be a family. Now, I just feel alone. I miss her."

Khan didn't reply right away because he had no idea how to handle this. His dad was either shouting and fussing or belittling him and being verbally abusive. This guy, the one who sounded broken and nostalgic, left him speechless. His father wasn't totally alone. His sister Lorelai lived abroad. Aunt Lorelai offered to help raise him, but his dad flipped, mostly because her husband was Afro-Latino.

Additionally, Khan's maternal uncle, his mom's younger brother, Cohen, lived in Texas. He also offered to take Khan why his father grieved, but his dad declined his help, too. Even after all these years, he didn't know why. "Well, Pop, we can be happy again. Maybe you should try reaching out to Uncle Cohen or Aunt Lorelai. We can have a little gathering and reconnect." His father grunted in response, and Khan could hear his shuffling in the background.

"I dunno."

"Well, think about it, Pop. My food I ordered just arrived. Would you like me to bring you something back to eat?"

"I don't care. I gotta go too."

Before he could reply, his father hung up the phone, and he headed back to the table. The party of three were having a deep discussion that stopped when he arrived.

"We were waiting for you before we started to eat the appetizer," Nehemiah stated.

"Thanks," he replied as he sat down beside Royale, who looked a tad upset, so he asked her what was wrong.

"It's nothing really. Kisha is being overly protective."

"I'm not. Listen, Khan, she's going to Philly, to the University of Pennsylvania for graduate school. That's awesome and all, but she wants to leave after church Sunday to drive to Philly all by herself. The worst part is, she has no place to live. Like, who goes to a state with no family, friends, or living arrangements." Kisha shook her head like a disapproving mother. "I've told you about making emotional decisions."

"Is that true?" Khan asked. Unbeknownst to the others, he and Royale talked on the phone a lot. He liked the cadence of her voice. It was soft and melodic like his mother's, and she was genuine. He missed that in women. He was surrounded by people who allowed their hate to consume them and thought the color of their skin made them better than others.

"Yes. I've more than overstayed my welcome with your family, Kisha. Your dad is coming back from his long-haul truck driving and I'm sure he doesn't want an extra person in his house."

"He doesn't care. As soon as he comes back home, Nehemiah will go back to his own apartment. He just stays with Momma and me while Daddy is on the road."

"That's true," Nehemiah added with a mouth full of food.

"Well, if you really want to go, then I'll go too. That way, you won't be all alone in the big city," Khan replied and quickly noticed the looks on both Kisha and Nehemiah's faces. Yeah, their wheels were turning, but he didn't care.

"You'd do that?"

He nodded he would.

"I see. Mmhm!" Kisha exclaimed, just as the waitress arrived with their entrees. "Y'all got something going on that I don't know about? I swore y'all just met two seconds ago."

Khan and Royale both ignored her. There was no talking once their food arrived. Royale extended her hands, prompting everyone else to do the same, and they all bowed their heads as she said grace. For some reason, that made Khan like her even more. His mom did the same thing. No matter what she was eating, she always told him to give thanks to God for everything, big and small.

While eating, Khan's cellphone went off again. This time, it was a text message.

Unknown: UR N2 black girls now?

Khan: Who is this?

Unknown: Oh, so you deleted my #. It's Everleigh!

Khan: Who I choose to spend my time with is my prerogative. I owe you no explanation.

After that, he blocked her number, and when he looked up, all six eyes were on him. He apologized for the interruption.

Thirty minutes later, they pulled up at Momma Byse's house and Khan got out first to open the door for both Kisha and Royale. As he was about to walk them inside, Nehemiah called him aside.

"What's up?"

"Dude, what're you doing? Nehemiah asked.

Khan frowned, confused. "Man, what are you talking about?"

"Khan, you and I know how your dad is. He barely tolerated me as your roommate. Remember how he showed out? Do you think if he finds out you are interested in a black woman, he'll just let that go? Technically, your dad is part of a domestic terrorist group. Those right-wing extremists your dad calls friends are crazy. He's crazy, which is why he's no longer a police officer. Royale has been through it, don't add to her heartbreak."

"It won't be like that," Khan defended.

"You just told me the man convicted of murdering your mother is getting a new trial, so Ronald is already in that kind of mood. Then, you know Heather and Everleigh are going to tell him everything they know and don't know. They're all members of that Christian Identity group. I swear, man, you're my brother, but if your daddy and his racist roadies come through harassing my family our friendship won't keep me from going blow to blow like it did when he called me the N-word back in college."

Khan exhaled heavily. He hadn't forgotten the verbal attacks his friend had faced because they chose to keep their friendship from high school well into college, and after. Nothing Nehemiah said was untrue, but he was so tired of his father's beliefs impacting his life. "I like her, Ne. I know I shouldn't because of what you said, but I can't help it. I don't even know her that well and I want to protect her and know everything about her. She's sweet and caring like my mom. She's thoughtful, funny, open and intelligent. Like, she's the perfect woman for me. I feel it."

"She's also black, which will cause you more harm than good. Honestly, both of you got a lot going on. Khan, at the end of the day, your dad is a violent racist associated with groups that commit hate crimes. It won't end well for you if you try to date her and be in your father's life. Somebody will get hurt."

"I know."

"So, you'll back off? Neither of you needs the extra stress that comes along with being an interracial couple. It's just too dangerous."

"Calm down, Ne, you're jumping ahead of yourself. I like her, and I won't let my pop's beliefs interfere with my life. I'm going to pursue her, and I won't let anything happen to her."

"I hear what you're saying, but you're living in a fantasy world. Don't be naïve about this. As your best friend I'm not sugarcoating anything. If you pursue her, then you must cut off all association with your father. He's too deep in his hate to ever change. You and I know just being friends with me is dangerous." He sighed before saying, "You need to pray on that decision."

Khan nodded his head in agreement. Maybe he was naïve, but he wasn't going to close the door on her, not even for his father. For some reason, he was willing to fight any battle and put out any flame just to have Royale in his life.

CHAPTER 7

Royale watched out the window, wondering silently to herself what Khan and Nehemiah were discussing. At times, it seemed civil, and then it seemed to get spirited only to relax again. She shook her head and let the curtain fall.

"Are you spying?" Kisha questioned.

"I was," she confessed with a smile.

Just as Kisha started to reply, Royale's cellphone went off. She glanced down at the screen and saw that it was Rina. She excused herself and quickly answered.

"Hello, Rina."

"Royale, you need to come home."

"I'm not coming back. I plan to stay here through Sunday, then leave to go to school and find a place to stay and get settled."

"Listen, my mom overheard our conversation, and then she told Dad, who told the General. Who demanded I contact you and tell you to come home. You know I can't say no to the General."

"Why the urgency?"

"Mom knows about your anxiety attacks, so I have to give them an expected time of arrival or the General is sending the freaking Black Ops for you."

Royale sighed in defeat. She'd been naïve to think she could slip away again after she had pulled the escape to Nairobi. "Tell them Sunday."

"I will, and I'm sorry."

"It's okay. I should have known my run would be short-lived. It's not like my grandfather can't find me. I swear this family has too many connections."

"I'll pass the information along, but how is Charming?"

That made Royale giggle. After she'd told Rina about Khan, she'd started calling him Charming. "We all went to a movie and out to eat tonight. I think he might like me, like, maybe more than friends, but I don't know."

"Well, I'm all for making friends, but you don't need to go beyond that. What's his entire name so I can do an internet search? We all know you are anti-internet."

"I'm not, I just couldn't deal with the trolls. Besides, sometimes it's better to ignore than to explore. Anyway, his name is Khan Masterson."

"Ha-ha, where did you get that from? It sounds like an Instagram meme."

"You know me. Look, tell everyone I'll be home Sunday evening after church."

"I sure will. I love ya."

"Love you, too, girlie!" Then they hung up.

Royale shook her head. She really had no desire to return home. Yeah, she was running from the issue, but who wanted to walk back into that drama? There was so much going on, and she didn't want to deal with it. She wasn't the one who had broken the family. That was all on her vessel, and that woman needed to accept responsibility for her actions and the family needed to let Royale deal with her pain the way she wanted, but that would never happen. It was time for closure, and when she left Virginia, this time to pursue graduate school, she was not returning. Virginia was her past, and one could never grow or survive in the past.

◆ ◆ ◆

"Well, Rina, what did she say?"

Rina turned around and looked at her mother. Even though she was petite, she had a way about her that made her seem like a giant. She could be imposing and gentle all at once, something she had perfected after Rina's biological father left their lives.

"She's coming home Sunday after church," Rina assured.

"Good, I'll call Grayling with the update. He has been a complete and utter mess since the incident, and then that visit with Royce just took him out." She shook her head before adding, "I guess you're going to your Bible Study group tonight?"

"Not tonight, I'm just going to stay in."

"Okay then."

Rina watched her mom leave, then opened her Surface Book and went straight to Google. She needed to know who this Khan Masterson was. She was all excited about Royale finding someone new to befriend because Matan had her all the way messed up, and that stunt he'd pulled at Starbucks was just unnecessary. Just as she had that thought, her cellphone started ringing. She rolled her eyes but answered.

"What do you want?"

"Rina, so glad you answered. If you aren't too busy, I'd like to meet with you tonight. I know it's short notice, but I have to catch the red-eye tonight. Anyway, I really wanted to speak with you in person before I go." His high, nasal voice was so annoying, and it always went up a higher octave when he was trying to get his way.

"Why me?"

"Just come meet me at The Hay-Adams, sweetie. Once you're here, we can discuss why you. Okay?"

Rina wasn't so sure about that, but she wondered just want he wanted, so she agreed to meet him. She'd just have to research Khan Masterson another time. She grabbed her jacket and keys and headed out. She knew her mother would wonder where she was heading, and she honestly didn't want to tell her the truth. So, once she was down the stairs, she simply told her that one of her friends had called and wanted to have a late dinner and she'd be back home soon.

It didn't take long for her to arrive. Rina wasn't really dressed to have a meeting. She wore a basic V-neck fitted shirt and gray leggings, showcasing her pear shape figure. When she entered the hotel's restaurant, she noticed Marc right away. He was easy to spot. He was dark chocolate with a bald head, and very metrosexual. He was always in whatever was fresh off the runway and loved his man purse, but he was one hundred percent straight.

"Rina, over here, dear," he called out.

She nodded and walked to the table. "What's so important that I needed to get here so quickly?"

Rina eyed him curiously as a sly smile seized his face, and he reached out his well-manicured hand to place on top of hers. Their eyes met as he finally opened his mouth in dramatic style. "Get on with it, Marc, and remove your hand from mine," she stated forcefully.

He did. "Oh, Rina, I liked the quiet you so much better. Anyway, I have an idea I want to pitch to you. I was thinking with all this going on with Royce, how about you and Royale get your own show. People love you girls. Now, before you say no, just listen to me.

"I'm thinking we call it *The Ruths*, *The Marys* or *Daughters of Disciples*, and then your storyline would be on how you're dealing with your father leaving—"

Rina put up her hand to halt him from speaking any more stupidity. "Stop right there. The only father I have is Bishop Grayling Chastain, and he isn't going anywhere," she interrupted.

"Sweetheart, you didn't let me finish. Now, like I was saying, we can discuss your biological father and how Bishop Chastain stepped up to the plate, how your parents' divorce impacted you, and maybe throw in some therapy sessions. People love that. Then, for Royale, I was thinking we follow her and her mom and how they rebuild their relationship after the Matan affair. Also, why does she refer to her Aunt Gwendolyn as 'Ma'? I just personally want to know."

Rina leaned back in her seat, giving Marc an incredulous and disapproving glare. He had really lost his mind with that one. There was so much wrong in what he was requesting. She just shook her head, face flushed with anger and agitation, her emerald eyes steely and dangerous. She would never do a reality show or see her biological father again. "No."

"But listen, I've reached out to Strom Evans just to test the waters and he was game. I also reached out to Matan and his mother, Roslyn. Well, I had to go through her to get to him, but they're on board. He really wants to get his side of the story out," Marc shared, apparently not at all affected by the various levels of lividness Rina was currently displaying.

"You. Did. What?" she quivered, tears now threatening to fall at his admittance. There were few people or things that scared her. However, she was bone-deep terrified of her biological father, who was a disturbed and cruel man. He beat not only her mother, but also her, and had even put hands on Royale. Only God in heaven knows how he'd escaped with his life after what he did. That was one time Grayling didn't think what would Jesus do; he thought what would a hoodlum do.

Anyway, Strom Evans was the worst of the worse because not only was he an abuser, but he was a bigamist who had another family. He had a white family back in West Virginia where he now resided. So, she had no use for him, no questions to be answered, and no wrong to right, he simply didn't exist. "How could you do that, and why would you? Does my mom know about this? Does Aunt Royce know about this? Why? You can't be serious." Her voice elevated, causing the patrons around them to look at her strangely, but she didn't care. This was crazy. She was shaking now. Would *he* attempt to contact her? Why would *he* want to even be on a reality show knowing the monstrous carnage he had left behind? It didn't make sense.

"Calm down, Czarina, just calm down. I wasn't trying to get you all emotional. It's an idea, a very good one that could make you lots of money. I know Bishop Chastain doesn't want to be on television. Right now, your Aunt Royce's therapists aren't sure she should revise her role while she is recuperating, even though that's what she wants. At any rate, the public and fans are hungry for something. You're like the Christian Kardashians; you're beautiful, rich and connected."

At that insult, Rina rolled her eyes hard. No real woman or Christian woman wanted to be associated with that mess of a family, not that she was judging, but really. Her family wasn't hungry for fame or money. "That is an offensive comparison, Marc. When did being a Kardashian become a standard to obtain? In fact, this entire pitch is offensive. Shame on you for even thinking it," she fussed, before continuing. "Whatever! Let's just get to the point, you called me because you believe I'm the weakest family member and that I would be Hello Kitty giddy to be the star of a spinoff reality show, right? I'm not. It's infuriating and shameful that you, Marcus Jeremy Perkins, would think I would ever consider this puerile pitch. No one in my family wants to be a part of it," she snapped, balling her fists and crashing them down onto the table for emphasis, sending silverware and empty wine glasses crashing around them.

The stunned appearance on his face was enough satisfaction for her. No one expected her to stand up for herself. Most of the time, she was fine playing the background and didn't care for the limelight, which gave people a false sense of security to try her. Well, not today. She feared Strom, but not anybody else.

"Well then, I see you are exasperated. I was only trying to help, but okay. How about you think it over and talk to Royale, then get back to me next week." He smiled, then waved at the waiter.

Rina was done. Marc was an inconsiderate butthole, and she wasn't going to entertain his tomfoolery any longer. The answer would always be no, and he couldn't wear her down to a yes. She popped out the chair so fast and hard, she nearly knocked down a passing patron and quickly apologized. Then she headed for the exit, leaving Marc by himself. As soon as she arrived outside, she called Grayling. He wouldn't be happy about this, and she knew it.

♦ ♦ ♦

Matan stared into nothingness. He couldn't believe the turn his life had made. He never meant to hurt Royale, he wanted to marry her, but her mother…the woman was an evil beauty. She was a satanic seductress who lured him in, only to spew him out. He was sure that she had somehow planned for them to get caught that night.

She ruined him.

He thought he was imagining things when she would give him longing looks or accidentally touch him, until one day, she kissed him. A kiss that was delicious and exquisite and left him thirsting for more. That kiss, that one kiss had turned his entire world upside down, and after that, he was a slave to her command. Whatever she wanted, he did, all while praying Royale never found out.

Then, six months into the relationship, his priorities were conflicted. He was attending theology school with the hopes of transferring to a school in Boston because he knew Royale was applying to schools there. However, what she didn't know was that her mother was taking up so much of his time, his grades were slipping in school. He tried to end it, but Royce threw the biggest hissy fit and threatened to tell Royale and Grayling about the affair, so he gave in. He wished he hadn't.

Then, somewhere around month eight, he fell in love with her and she became his obsession. He was fixated on pleasing her and he got sloppy about who saw them and where they met. It was like they wanted to get caught, but when they finally did, when he saw the hurt on Royale's face before she fainted, that nearly killed him. It was like the spell he was under had completely vanished. He realized he wasn't in love with Royce; he was just in lust.

Once Royale ran off to Nairobi and Royce went running to rehab, everyone believed Royce to be a victim and him a villain. It was then he came to see how truly evil she was. Her ability to manipulate was uncanny. The woman was bewitching. She was a gorgeous woman, but she was haughty.

She could be a chameleon with the way she could blend in with her surroundings, but she was as deadly and dangerous as a Komodo dragon. Her bite was most definitely poisonous. Now he knew what he was working with, and it wasn't worth what he had lost. Royale loved him. She was dedicated, honest, pure and sincere. Honestly, she and Grayling were the true victims of his and Royce's sins.

He had no reason to go to another woman, especially her mother, but the sex had lulled him. He'd been controlled by his flesh and not by his faith, and he'd faltered and failed. Now that he realized life had no meaning without the woman he loved, he was breaking and desperate. That brokenness and desperation led him to act a fool in Starbucks and get into a shoving match with a Fetty Wap wannabe.

"Matan, baby, what'cha doing out here all alone?" Roslyn asked.

"Just thinking, momma, and wishing I'd acted differently." He sighed heavily before confessing what was really on his mind. "I miss Royale, momma. I took her love for granted, and now I yearn for it. I miss the closeness I had with her family. Well, not her mother. I don't miss that woman, but I miss…"

"It's okay, baby. Things will get better. Have you considered what Marc said about the show? That could help you get Royale back. Think about it. Think about the money you'd make being one of the stars."

Matan shook his head. He would do the show if Royale did it. If the show would bring her back to him, then absolutely, but if not, he wasn't interested. He was catching enough flack as it was and didn't necessarily want to be on television for the world to judge. Black Twitter was going in on him hard after the Starbucks incident because he came off as uppity and disgraceful for the way he expressed himself. "Maybe, momma."

"Well, the lawyer contacted me today, and guess what? He thinks we have a good suit. Royce pretty much seduced you, then Grayling turned his back on you and ruined your good name all because Royce didn't want you to marry her daughter. It's defamation of character, pain and suffering, and the list goes on."

Matan loved his mother, but none of what she said was defamation of character. True, there was pain and suffering, but at his own hands. The truth of the matter was, he did have an affair with his mentor's wife. Yeah, Royce made him out to look like the one who had pursued her, but at the end of the day, they had both sinned and were both wrong. It seemed to him, even after all her deception, Royce took the bigger hit. Those same people bashing him were now bashing her because she was twice his age. He was sure his momma had orchestrated the release of the tapes that unfavorably showcased Royce. He was sure she was behind the Twitter campaign that bashed Royce too. Still, he accepted his role. "No lawsuit, momma. I was wrong. If you pursue this, they may countersue. We can't afford that, so just let it go."

"You were seduced and misled by an older woman. She set you up. Now she's in therapy, hogwash. She's an old-school whore, been getting down since the 80s. You know, Grayling was supposed to be your daddy, but she came in with all her hips, hotness, and high dollar clothing having a copious of boys drooling over her like Bernese Mountain dogs.

"She took my boyfriend. She just stole Grayling from me. She loved attention then, just like she loves it now. She's always coming for what belongs to me! We're suing her. Even if it can't be for defamation, I'll get her for something. She deserves to be punished for what she did to us, well, you," she scoffed.

Matan turned his dark brown eyes to his mother, and he knew she had gone back in time. He never got the full story about her, Grayling and Royce, but he knew the women fake-liked each other. They said all the customary conversational words, but they weren't truly friends. They were more like frenemies. He also knew his mother had tried to offer herself to Grayling, and prior to that, she used his relationship with Grayling to get closer to him. Matan's middle name was a variation of Grayling. His mother had named him Graymond, and he always wondered about how his biological father and Grayling felt about that. However, Matan never had the courage to ask. He believed in his momma really thought he was the son Grayling never had. Now, he had ruined that relationship too.

"Momma, don't you think it's better to pray for her than to prey on her? I was in the wrong. I should have stopped it, but I allowed myself to give into my carnal thoughts. Yes, she is twice my age and should have never come on to me, but I didn't have to reciprocate. I should have man-up and gone to Bishop Grayling and talked to him or one of the other associate pastors, and I didn't. I should've never crossed that line. Bishop Grayling, Gwendolyn, and my Royale were beyond good to me, and I repaid their love with betrayal. I won't sue that woman. I'll just let God handle it. All I want to do now is get Royale back."

"I pray you do get Royale back. I love her like a daughter, I do. I hate how she's been hurt by all this foolishness. However, I called Grayling, and he pretty much let me know that he wasn't going to help us. He told me I needed to speak to the other ministers in the church because he was taking a leave of absence. That didn't sit well with me, especially when I felt like he was putting all the blame on you. It's all just a pile of crock because he wants to wash his hands of us."

Matan smirked, hearing his mother say a pile of crock. She was a God-fearing woman, but she cursed like no tomorrow until she started being around Royale, who never cursed. A pile of crock was one of her favorite phrases, and it was cute to hear his momma say it. Shaking his head, he knew he had it bad for Royale. He needed to see her again and work things out.

"Momma, I know you're upset, but bringing a lawsuit won't help, and if Bishop Grayling told you he's taking a leave of absence, then he is. The man has been through an ordeal that any other would have probably killed me over. Respect the fact that he needs to find peace and get back to God so he can lead his flock forward. Don't jump to the conclusion that he has washed his hands of us, he just needs time."

"Hump! Well, since you're all wise, where were those pearls of wisdom when you started messing about with Royce? Where was this wisdom a few days ago when you were in Starbucks, accosting Royale and that thug? Sometimes, boy, I swear you act like your good for nothing, incarcerated father."

For him, it was the moment in Starbucks that finally opened the floodgates of his foolish behavior. He had hit rock bottom because he wasn't a violent man. Sometimes cocky, and a bit of a showoff, but never violent. "I don't know, momma. Look, I need to head home. I love you," he told her and kissed her forehead, purposely not responding to the invective statement she made about him being like his absentee father. He was sure she knew that her slip of the tongue had offended him. It wasn't her comparison to his father that upset him, it was the fact that she pretended as if his father was the worst man alive. After hugging her, he quickly gathered his belongings, got into his car and headed home, blasting Andy Mineo.

When he entered his apartment, he dropped his keys, kicked off his dress shoes and flopped down on the sofa. Instead of reaching for the television remote to lose himself in some comedy, he grabbed his cellphone and called Rina. Hopefully, she would accept his call because he didn't have Royale's new number, and he wouldn't dare call Grayling's landline. So, the only person he could contact was Rina, but the phone just kept ringing. She must have blocked him. He slumped his shoulders and dropped his head. He could feel the beginnings of a major headache. It was like all the tension in his body was going to his head. He hated being this way. He was a mess and depressed. Times like these, he needed Royale. She'd tell him to calm down, massage his shoulders and hum him some cute little tune. She had the voice of seven angels. She could out sing her grandmother, and that woman was a lyrical legend.

"Yo, Tan, I didn't hear you come in. You got a message from ol' girl," Fontaine, his roommate, told him.

Just like that, life came back into Matan's slumped body. "Royale called me?"

"Nah, the other one, Royce."

"What? What did she want?" he asked, sitting up on the couch, the stressful tension returning at being informed that Royce had phoned him. They weren't to have any contact, per him. He wanted nothing to do with her. He looked at Fontaine, who was pouring himself some orange juice and peeling a banana before acknowledging Matan's inquiry.

"Just that she needs to see you. She said she called your cellphone, but assumed you had blocked her. Anyway, she did sound urgent, but if I was you, I'd avoid that siren at all cost. Can't nothing good come from seeing that woman. She already messed you up once, so I would suggest you ignore her," Fontaine advised.

"Probably got something to do with my mom trying to sue the Chastains."

"What? Why Ma Ros wanna be messy like that?"

"Revenge, pettiness, just outright can't stand the woman. My momma and Royce got an old-school beef, and I'm in the middle." He didn't tell his friend that he thought his mom had used him too. More than likely, his mother had pushed him and Royale together, because if she couldn't get Grayling as a husband, she could have him as an in-law. The more he thought about it, the more it made sense. Royce had used him to hurt his mother, but in the process, she had hurt her daughter and husband. However, she had gotten her end result, which was to break them up.

Poor Royale was just collateral damage, a casualty of a war she knew nothing about. The more he thought about it, the angrier he became. The affair was never about him. Royce didn't love him. She might've lusted for him, but it was never love. The affair, in his mind, was about two women who both wanted the same man and used their children as pawns for their own gain. In the process, they had ruined innocent lives. How had he not seen it before? Why hadn't he had that insight in the beginning. He was so dumb a year ago, and now he saw it all clearly. He was too caught up getting the goodies to see the storm brewing. Now his entire life was out for the world to view and judge, but worse of all, he had lost the one woman he loved and possibly his career.

Fontaine nodded. "Don't get cooked," he joked.

"Right? These women are ruining me. Man, for real, I'm tired and worn. I don't know how much more I can take."

"Man, you sound like that song "Worn" by Tenth Avenue North. But listen, maybe you need to take off. Let's do a man trip and get outta the area. We can go to Myrtle Beach, or check out Charleston, SC. They got some nice places, and we can rent a yacht and go sailing. Or how about Vermont? You know, I've always wanted to go to Vermont. That looks like a peaceful place, and bruh, you need a peaceful place to hang. No moms, no exes, no cells, just chill."

"That sounds nice. Maybe if I can clear my mind, I can get back to the me I used to be before I lost everything."

"You will, and eventually, Royale will forgive you. Just give her some space, then talk to her. Let her know your side and be prepared for her animosity. Lord knows that girl loved you and she loved you hard. So, her witnessing you smashing her moms had to be difficult," Fontaine stated as he pushed up his glasses and placed his empty glass in the sink.

That was why he liked Fontaine. He was just real. He stood an even six feet and was lanky, but the girls loved him. Unlike Matan, he came from a two-parent home, but his parents were atheists. However, Fontaine had joined the church two years ago, and it was because of Royale. He said he liked how she wasn't judgmental nor did she try to pour Christianity down his throat. Instead, she led by example, and that had an impact on Fontaine.

During the time Matan was stepping out on Royale, he and Fontaine's relationship suffered. Eventually, Fontaine forgave him, and Matan hoped Royale and her family would forgive him also.

"You right, let's ride out, but not Vermont. Maybe like Las Vegas or San Diego."

"Whatever, works for you. I'll call some of the frat to link up with us."

Matan nodded in agreement. That was what he needed. He needed to get away from everything and everyone and have a moment to chill and think. He also needed to have a long talk with God because he needed some counseling and direction, and he wasn't sure where to get that now that Grayling was out of his life.

CHAPTER 8

Ronald sat at his computer at the training compound, updating the website for his white pride page. This was one of his two jobs since he was no longer a police officer. He did the web page and was the lead strategist for the Klan Bureau of Investigation. The KBI was pioneered by the Mississippi White Knights, and they incorporated it into their group to investigate Klan enemies, leaks and to identify any undercovers. He didn't do the physical part of it due to the progression of his OA, but he was still vital to the team. There were infiltrators at every corner, and it was his duty to find them when he wasn't drunk. He was doing well until he learned about Kalid getting a new trial. Shaking the thought, he pulled himself back to the job at hand.

He was attempting to increase their membership by making their web page more interactive for the tweens and teens. It was never too early to prepare them for the race war he knew was coming. They believed if they could get the young, they could raise an army of warriors. One way to lure a younger crowd was through social media and music, and that was exactly what he was doing. It was a shame that he could reach other people's children, but not his own.

Ronald believed where he went wrong with Khan was by taking his grief of losing his wife out on his son. He beat the crap out of Khan, and the boy never gravitated to his way of thinking, but it wasn't too late to turn him. Even before his wife was murdered, he had a friend who turned him onto the beliefs of the Christian Identity. The Christian Identity helped guide him. They were classified as a hate group, but, in actuality, it was a religion that believed whites, not Jews, were the true Israelites favored by God in the Bible.

He and other members affiliated with the religion believed Jews were biologically descended from Satan. Additionally, non-whites were soulless *mud people* and the *mutts* (biracial abominations) created with the other Biblical *beasts of the field*. Being part of the Christian Identity ideology, he had already known that whites were superior, but after a black man murdered his wife, it was an easy decision to join the KKK and recruit others to follow.

It was necessary for his survival and way of life to be around individuals who understood his pain and anger. He didn't believe they were domestic terrorists. In fact, they were a brotherhood seeking to live their life the way God intended. They were the rightful descendants and wouldn't allow the muddies to overtake their religion or way of life. The terrorist in his mind were the Black Separatist, those crazies chanting that black lives matter, and those uppity pastors who blamed the white man for all the bad things that happened to black people. If they just stayed in their place, white people wouldn't have to keep putting them there.

The media was so biased. It never reported on the Black Separatist, but they were always on the white supremacy groups like they were an abomination to mankind. The Black Separatist opposed integration and racial intermarriage and wanted separate institutions. Some even advocated for a separate nation for blacks. If they wanted to go back to Africa, then he was all for it. He was Team Black Exodus out of America; now that would make America great again. The Jews, Latino/as, and mutts could leave, too, and they'd have a pure America. A beautiful, white America. That was the *American Dream*. The idea of that made him giddy inside. He found himself smiling. He was so wrapped up in his warped sense of reality, he hadn't noticed he had a visitor until she called out.

"Mr. Masterson?"

Ronald looked up from the computer to find Heather standing before him. "What'chu need, sweetheart?"

"Well, I wanted to talk to you about Khan."

Ronald stopped what he was doing and gave her his full attention. He hoped she was over her crush because Khan wasn't the least bit interested, and he wasn't going to force the boy to take her. As much as he liked her family, she wasn't the one for Khan. Now, Everleigh, on the other hand, he liked for his son. Heather was a sweet girl, but as far as looks go, she wasn't the most attractive. She had one of those faces only a mother and father could love. "What's going on?"

"I saw him earlier this week with them black people. It looked like he was on a date with one of 'em. Everleigh tried to talk to him, but he was dismissive. I just thought you should know the kind of company he's entertaining. I know due to his landscaping business he interacts with the inferior, but he don't gotta be dating 'em. We don't believe in interracial relationships. That's an abomination, and he should know better."

Ronald placed his thumb and index finger over the bridge of his nose and shook his head in shame. She was correct, his son knew better, but he had suspected Khan was doing this to get back at him. Khan's actions were embarrassing him and could jeopardize his position, so he needed to get a handle on the situation. It was one thing to work for those kind, and he knew because he had to fake it while he was a police officer. However, to actually go out in public on a date with a darkie was going too far. He knew Khan was up to something, but he didn't know it was that. "I'll talk to him, thanks for letting me know."

"You're welcome," she replied and walked back out of his office.

If the Imperial Grand Wizard found out about his son, he wondered how he would react. He knew they would question his effectiveness and wonder if he couldn't get his son to join the movement, how would he be able to recruit others? Here he was, the tactician for the KBI, but didn't know his son was moonlighting with the enemy.

He was sure the Byse family had something to do with it. That, or his sister Lorelai or his deceased wife's brother, Cohen. They were simpletons who believed in the integration of all the races and believed that God didn't intend for one race to dominate the other, but that was all lies. Somebody had to lead, and that had always been and always would be the white man.

Acts 17:26 showcased that and Bob Jones Sr. had it right. It was a shame when Bob Jones University was forced to integrate back in 1971. It was the school Ronald's father had attended, and so had he. Sadly, the school backed off the belief of the founder, but it didn't matter, the truth was the truth. The Bible didn't lie. It was in Genesis 4 that God placed a visible mark on Cain, the "Mark of Cain", for killing his brother, Abel. Cain lied to God when God inquired what happened. Ronald interpreted it as the fifth century Christians did, that the curse was black skin, and therefore slavery was justified. Not only that, it was necessary.

Furthermore, the Bible speaks of the *Curse of Ham* which justified slavery, and some of Ronald's fellow brothers believed that when Noah and his family were on the ark, the entire family was white, therefore, any blacks had to be among the animals. That made sense because blacks acted like a bunch of animals, maybe worse than that. He had more respect for a mutt, flea-infested dog than a black person, especially since his wife was dead because of one. That information was what they would use as a rallying cry at the upcoming Klan rally. They were having a small get-together, something like an interest meeting, which was another reason why he was updating the website.

Ronald needed to quickly finish so he could talk to Khan. It was time for him to make up his mind. Either he was going to embrace his father's beliefs, or Ronald was going to disown him. He'd let the boy have a black roommate, he allowed him to hang out with others, but now it was time to embrace his whiteness and privilege. His son could become a Grand Wizard one day. He had a spark and ease about him that made people want to follow him, and Ronald wanted him to use it to unite the whites and rule over the blacks.

♦ ♦ ♦

Khan struggled to wake up. He was so tired, and his mind was plagued by visions of his mother's murder. That happened when he was stressed. Yesterday had been stressful and brutal because he had somehow overbooked himself and his crew. By the grace of God, they got it all done, even though they all had to work overtime.

Khan was mad that he hadn't gotten to talk to Royale or Honey Drop, as he liked to call her because it made her blush. She had come to his job and brought him chicken dumplings and biscuits with a gallon of sweet tea. That was all it took for a simple man like him. But due to his schedule, he had missed their nightly phone call. It surprised him how in just a few days, she'd become as necessary as the air he breathed. He didn't know how it had happened, but she was all-consuming, and for the life of him, he couldn't understand how her ex-boyfriend didn't see that.

Plus, they had the best conversation, never at a loss for words or topics, and she just made him feel alive again. It was like when she came into his life, she hit the reset button, and he loved that. He had even called his cousin Canton to tell him about her, and he wanted to meet her. Even with the mess about the man who might've killed his mother circulating, he was calm because he had Royale's friendship.

"Khan, boy, you up?"

"Yeah, Pop," he replied sleepily. He was mad his pop was interfering his thoughts of Royale.

"Good, we need to talk." He heard his father mumble as his footfalls neared his bedroom. He watched his father enter his bedroom and he had on nothing but boxer shorts, his pale, hairless chest looked sunken, but his eyes were full of life. He was surprised his father hadn't been drinking, and that could only mean there was something about to go down. His father liked to be alert when his friends had their little social hour.

"What's on your mind?" he queried, as he rubbed the sleep out of his eyes. His muscled body slowly unwound as he turned his attention toward the bedroom door where his father stood to his full size, eyes steady and serious, looking squarely into his. The question he'd asked his father, he already knew the answer, but he played dumb. It had been two days since he'd run into Heather and Everleigh, and he was sure one, if not both, had ratted him out.

"Where did I go wrong? Why do you hate being white so much that you'd purposely go against my beliefs and prance around town with them black people? You think they care about you? They come from the same cursed tribe as the man who killed your mother. Blacks are murderers and they even kill each other. Now, you're out there hanging with them when you need to be supporting your own kind. So, tell me, where did I go wrong, and how can I make it right?"

Khan just glared at his father in shock. Usually, he was shouting and calling him boy and telling him he was a loser, a weakling or calling him stupid and soft. He knew how to deal with angry Ronald, but not vulnerable Ronald. He looked almost pitiful, as if it truly pained him that Khan wasn't like him. "Pop, what are you talking about?"

"I'm talking about Heather seeing you with them blacks, and how rudely you treated her. I done told you to stay away from the Byse family. Consider them and all other blacks to be enemies. They ain't to be trusted. I don't know how it feels to witness your mother being murdered, but if it's making you sympathetic to them muddies, then you need to get professional help. We got our own therapist.

"However, if you're acting out to get back at me for how I treated you as a child, then you need to let that crap go. We're white people, and we don't mix, befriend or associate with the enemy. There's a reason they were enslaved to us. Now, stop this infatuation you have with them. I know their women are tempting because they look different, but don't be fooled, they're touched by the devil. You saw it yourself with that gal on the news. Her mother was having an affair with her boyfriend. That's what they do, just sick and sinful the lot of 'em," he lectured as he unfolded his arms.

"Now is the time for you to decide to stand on the side of justice with your mother and me or be with the enemy that killed your mother. I won't let you stay in my home while you're befriending the enemy unless it's for the cause and you're plotting to eliminate the threat. Is that what it is? You're undercover or, are you like my sister Lorelai? I won't have that in my home. You weren't raised to embrace them. So, decide now."

Khan shook his head. Here was the ignorant racist rearing his ugly head. He was so tired of hearing this same old crap. It was never anything new, and he didn't want to deal with it anymore. "Pop, I'll never be racist. I don't hate people. I hate that my mother was murdered, and I hate how that has altered your mind and damaged your soul; however, I won't embrace the racial prejudices and acrimony you have in your heart. I do business with everybody, and I attended college with all kinds of people, that's life. It doesn't have to be us against them.

"Every black man isn't a murderer and can't be blamed for mom's death. She wouldn't want this, Pop. She wouldn't," Khan lectured as he flipped the covers off his long, muscled legs, allowing them to hang over the mattress as his bare feet rested on the carpeted floor. "Pop, I'm not trying to get back at you. I just want us to be father and son. I moved back in because you asked me to help you since your arthritis is getting worse, but if you want me to move out, I will." He never took his eyes off his father, and by the reddening of his face, Khan knew he was hitting a sensitive area, but his father needed to hear the truth. "Pop, I vow this. I won't ever become a card-carrying member of the Klan, and I won't ever agree with the religious philosophy of the Christian Identity. I'll always love you, but I'll never become you. If that makes me like Aunt Lorelai or Uncle Cohen, then so be it.

"FYI, if you die today, Pop, and you went to Heaven, you'd be with all of God's people. There aren't separate heavens for the races, and there is no separate Hell either, so you might as well embrace the fact that the same Jesus who died on the cross for Jews and Gentiles, died for every race God created. Just because you don't like God's truth, doesn't negate it."

Before he could get up, his father was on him, hurling limp punch after limp punch. This man knew he had OA, and he also knew Khan wasn't a scared little boy anymore. He was a grown man, but he didn't want to hurt his father. "Pop, really, you need to stop. You're going to hurt yourself. There's no need to get violent. I said I'd move out," he replied without any exertion. His father wasn't physically hurting him at all, but he was pissing him off. He lifted his father up and slammed him on the bed. "Enough! I'm leaving, so just calm down."

"You're a disgrace, Khan. A freaking waste of egg and sperm. I swear God cursed me when He gave me you. I can't believe you came from my loins. You're a pitiful, powerless, pacifist play toy for them monkeys you love so much."

Monkeys? Not today. That was it. Before Khan realized what, he was doing, he had already knocked his father out cold. He pulled himself away, shocked by his reaction to his father's crass language, but he couldn't take it anymore. All he thought about was what Nehemiah had said. He couldn't continue to allow his father to speak such venom about people he loved. No more.

He quickly checked Ronald's pulse; the man was alive, good. He lifted him up and carried him back to his bedroom before returning to his own and packing up his bags. In the process, he phoned his cousin, Canton.

"What's up, K?" came his cousin's southern drawl. Canton spoke more with a southern accent, while Khan was all country.

"Canton, I finally did it. I just pounded the old man, now I'm moving out. He told me to either choose him and his beliefs or he'd disown me, and I chose to be disowned. I can't live my life like that anymore."

"Dude, did you just say you knocked out your dad?" he asked with humor in his tone.

"Yeah. He found out about my date or not a date with Royale. You know how he feels about interracial dating. The Byse family has been good to me, and Royale has known me for less than a week and treats me like royalty. I've lived with my dad my entire life and he treats me like trash. I was holding onto him because he's the only parent I have left, but I can't anymore. He loves to hate, and I no longer want to be part of his misery, so, I'm disowning him."

"I'm coming up there. You know he'll try something stupid. Let me tell my dad and send me an address to where you'll be. I don't trust Uncle Ronald, especially when he's in his drunk, emotional state of mind. He whines worse than that rapper Drake after a breakup. You know he's been on the ready ever since he found out about the new trial, so just leave now before things get out of hand."

"All right, I have to go. Talk to you later," Khan replied and hung up as he resumed his packing.

By the time he was done, his father was rousing, but Khan ignored his mumbles and grumbles and headed to his truck. He'd left his work truck at work and only had his personal truck so he wouldn't have to return home. He loaded his truck, and it reminded him of when he first encountered Royale. She had her entire life in her SUV, fleeing from Virginia, from her past because of the pain, and in some ways, he was too. He should have left the trailer a long time ago, but better late than never. He got in his truck and took off, not even looking back. That was his past. He drove right over to the Byse family home. He needed to see Royale.

CHAPTER 9

Grayling sat gravely silent in deep rumination as Rina recounted her interaction with Marc. Apparently, he didn't take heed to Grayling's warning. He knew that people could be slimy and grimy as the young people would say. However, he had no idea Marc would go behind his back to meet with Rina. He was both irked and bewildered at the lengths Marc would go to satisfy his greed. If that wasn't enough, he had the other issue to deal with. Roslyn was seeking to sue because of what had happened between her son and his wife. He felt he would mentally erupt.

Grayling just needed a moment to deal because everything was coming at him all at once. As a pastor, he knew prayer was his most powerful tool, but that didn't make his anger yield. He had not expected for Marc to go against his wishes and disrespect him the way he had by coming for his family. A small part of him suspected that his wife might have been involved, but he didn't know. He would be sure to bring it up when he visited her again.

After exhaling a deep breath, he replied to Rina. "Sweetheart, you know that I'll not permit anything to happen to you or your mother. Strom will never be an issue because he knows that if he attempts to contact you, I'll use every connection to shut him down. Don't you worry about that, and as far as Marc goes, I'll handle him too. You need to change your cellphone number like Royale did. There won't be any more reality shows. So, don't stress over that. Okay?"

"Okay," she mumbled to him, but her slumped shoulders and quivering bottom lip indicated to him that everything wasn't okay. She was just pacifying him and he decided to address it.

"Czarina, look at me," he softly commanded. He knew her well. Rina was terrified of her biological father, and for good reason. Yet, he'd done his best to eliminate that fear, but Marc's careless actions had brought her worst nightmare to the forefront.

Her green eyes, eyes inherited from her Welsh father, found their way to his. He offered her an enduring smile. "Trust me, honey, when

I say that Strom won't hurt you again. I'm not letting anyone hurt you, Royale or Gwendolyn. That is my vow to you."

"I know, and I believe you, I'm just upset. I know he picked me because everyone thinks I'm weak. The internet trolls had a field day about my lack of black girl attributes and attitude. People think I'm too quiet and easy to get over on."

Grayling shook his head in dismay. He loathed social media and how it distorted the girls' views of themselves. "No, sweetheart, you aren't weak. You were in a bad situation that you survived. You're doing so many great things, don't let this set you back. We're going to get through this storm. Psalm 34:17 tells us *that when the righteous cry for help, the Lord hears and delivers them out of all their troubles.*"

She smiled. "Dad, that was my quiet time verse, so I know God wants me to hear it. Believe it or not, I know I'm not weak, I just have moments, and I shouldn't care what people perceive me to be because I know who God created me to be. Still, I just get so nervous when I hear his name. My body gets all cold and covered with goosebumps, and it's like instantly, I'm that scared little girl again, hiding from him while he hurts my momma. Why didn't he love us like he loved his white family?"

He didn't know the answer to her latter question, only Strom could answer that. "Come here, sweetheart." He motioned for her to sit on his lap and she did. He pulled her into his chest and held her. "What did I used to tell you when you were younger?"

"That God is with me wherever I go, and that all His children have angels, an entire army of them that protect us, me. When I feel scared, all I need to do is call out to Him. God will provide what I need when I need it. I should never be afraid because God said fear not. God is the truth, and if He tells us not to be afraid, then we shouldn't be."

"Right. The way Strom treated you and your mom was atrocious, but he has no power unless you grant it to him. Remember, what you have that he doesn't is God and His Army. Do not be afraid, God will give you what you need when you need it. Romans 8:26-28, *the Spirit helps us in our weakness. We do not know what we ought to pray for, but the Spirit Himself intercedes for us with groans that words cannot express. And he who searches our hearts knows the mind of the Spirit because the Spirit intercedes for the saints in accordance with God's will. And we know that in all things, God works for the good of those who love Him, who have been called according to His purpose.* When you feel afraid, lost, or worried, remember what we can't say, Christ can articulate and intercede on our behalf. You'll always be safe in God, and I'll always be here for you." He felt her let out a calm breath as she wrapped her arms around him.

"Thank you for being my uncle and my dad. I love you."

"I love you more. Now, come on, let's see if we can convince my sister to make us one of those chocolate chip pies."

"Okay."

◆ ◆ ◆

Royale was incensed as she read Rina's text about Marc, with his ol' metrosexual self. He was nothing more than Royce's patsy. He had no right to call a meeting with Rina to try and persuade her to do a reality show. Their family was in shambles, and he was wrong to take advantage and try to profit from their pain. He was a sneaky little worm, and once she got back to Virginia, she was going to give him a piece of her mind. He needed to see the other side of Royale Makeda Chastain.

"Royale, Khan is here!" Kisha shouted up the stairs.

Just like that, her anger shifted, and she calmed at Khan's arrival. Royale put down her cellphone and quickly looked in the mirror to fix herself. She was wearing yoga pants and a fitted V-neck charcoal gray shirt. She hadn't expected any company this early, but she headed downstairs anyway. Hopefully, he wouldn't notice her lazy look.

Last night Royale called him but was unable to talk to him. Then he hadn't texted her back when she woke up this morning, so she wondered if everything was okay. Royale hoped it was because she had limited mental space to deal with drama. Lord knows her cup was overflowing with it.

Royale bounced down the stairs with a look of consternation on her wheat toasted face. Her copper lit eyes captured his and instantly, she knew something was wrong. He wasn't his confident and charming self. His summer blue eyes were wild, and his pupils were dilated. It seemed that he still had his pajamas on, as he wore a basic white T-shirt paired with WVU pajama bottoms. His long hair was in disarray, some parts in a man bun, while other parts hung unrestrained. His overall appearance was a bit disheveled, and that was unlike Khan. He had his cowboy getup, his work outfit, and his urban style, but this was a first seeing him this way, unkempt. Something happened. "What's wrong, Khan? What happened?"

"Can we talk?" he asked.

There was a desperation in his plea that concerned her more. "Of course," she replied, giving Kisha a concerned glance as she followed him back out the door. They could have stayed in the house and had the same amount of privacy because only Kisha was home, but maybe Khan felt more comfortable outdoors.

As the two exited the door, Royale could tell Khan's mind was working overtime because when he was in deep contemplation, he got a little frown line across the top of his T-zone. They had spent a short amount of time together, but they talked every day and had grown close in the short time of meeting one another.

Royale honestly never thought she would feel comfortable around a man again, or even trust anyone after the betrayal of her mother and her ex. However, Khan was easy to care about and talk with. She needed to find out what had him upset. "Khan, you're gritting your teeth. What happened for you to be here and not at work?"

He let out a deep breath. "Pop and I got into a physical altercation because I refuse to live my life the way he wants. He told me either do as he says or leave his house. I chose to leave, and he chose to attack me. I didn't want to hurt him, but he just pushed the wrong button. He was coming to when I left, but I just got so mad." She knew he was angry because he had his fist tightly bound.

Taken aback by his confession, she quickly got over it and pulled him into a hug. He was a big guy, and much taller than her, but he fell into her embrace like a child in need of shelter. She wasn't fully aware of his situation with his father, but she knew his mother was dead, and his father was all he had. She hated that he had found himself in such a quandary with his father.

She rubbed the nape of his neck for a few seconds before breaking away. She looked at his face, but didn't see any bruises, then she checked his hands and saw how flaming red his left knuckles were. At that moment, something took over, and it was like an out-of-body experience as she lifted his left hand to her lips and kissed each knuckle. She had no idea what had possessed her to do that. As soon as she finished, he lifted his right hand and caressed her face, ending up under her chin. She watched with hungry anticipation as his plump, pink lips drew nearer to hers, imprisoning her. It was like New Year's Day and the Fourth of July had collided because there were so many sparks.

In that moment, everything was right, her past forgotten. Their lips crashed into each other and it was like an out-of-body experience. Royale lost herself in his kiss. His kisses were like balm to her hungry lips, releasing dormant desires that even Matan had never unlocked. Yet, it was all too soon. This wasn't supposed to be happening, and she shouldn't feel this connected to him, and yet, he was like her lifeline. She hadn't known him a week, and here she was, kissing him and being vulnerable. That was completely unlike her. He made her a contradiction, and it ignited and excited her.

Royale made Matan wait an entire year before she kissed him, but then, he did cheat on her, and for all she knew, he had been cheating their entire courtship. At some point, Khan stopped kissing her, but she still felt the warmness of him. Her eyes were still closed, and her lips puckered. It wasn't until he caressed her cheeks that she opened her eyes. "You kissed me."

"I've wanted to kiss you since you made me those cinnamon honey drop biscuits. I wanted to know if your lips tasted as good as those biscuits. Guess what, they taste better. Your lips even taste like cinnamon and honey."

She felt her flesh glow scarlet at his flirtatious comment. It seemed whenever she was in his presence, she was doomed to blush. It was so embarrassing. "I…I, we, well, you came here to talk, not to make out. I don't know what came over me. I apologize for my wanton actions."

"I came over here to feel better, and I feel so much better now. Don't apologize, and nothing about what just occurred was wanton. I like you a lot, Royale. It's not because you were on a reality show, or because I feel sorrow for what happened to you. I like you because when I look at you, when your eyes catch mine, I feel secure, hopeful, exhilarated and giddy. The chemistry between us is undeniable," he told her as his index finger traced the outer lines of her lips.

"After my mother was murdered, few things felt right or made me happy or feel safe. However, with you, I feel all of that. It's crazy because I only met you a few days ago, and yet, it feels like I've known you my entire life. I like the man I am with you. It just feels right. It feels fated, ordained, like God put you right in my path to show me that He still remembers me. My faith isn't as strong as yours. You can imagine how angry I was at God when He took my mom and left me with my dad. Ever since you arrived in my life, praying with me every night, not even knowing how your words gave me strength, has made me rekindle my dead faith."

She didn't see that coming, but that was the most beautiful thing he could say because her faith meter wasn't so high either. Whether he knew it or not, they were helping each other. She wrapped her hands around his massive arms, rubbing them as he held her face. She felt safe in his embrace, too, and if she were honest, her favorite place to be was in his arms with her head resting on his broad chest. It had only happened in her dreams, but seeing it come to fruition was thrilling.

Khan felt so different than Matan. The emotions and feelings he evoked were different. He set her soul afire. With him, nothing was forced or uncomfortable. Khan made her laugh and forget about the scandalous and hurtful behavior of her family. She could breathe with him. With Khan there was no suffocating feeling like she felt upon her return to Virginia. Best of all, he didn't trigger her anxiety attacks. In fact, he felt more like an antidote. He was correct in his assessment: they felt right together. Besides, he could rock a man bun better than Brock O'Hurn, but she still needed to play devil's advocate.

A weak heart was easily misled, and she didn't want to travel down the path of heartbreak again because she wasn't enough. She needed to be enough for him if they were ever going to be more than a moment. No matter how confident a woman may be, once she finds out her significant other is cheating, whether once or numerous times, it creates insecurity. However, she couldn't withhold the truth, her heart wouldn't allow it. "I like you, too, but you know with what has happened, the last thing I want is to hop from one relationship to another. Maybe this is all conjecture and you're only reacting to me in this way because of your highly emotional state. Neither of us deserves to be the other's rebound."

He shook his head in the negative. "I must say, I'm not surprised by your hesitation and concern. I appreciate you admitting your feelings. Now, let me tell you mine. You're not a rebound. I'm telling you how I feel now, and that won't change. If it makes you feel better, we'll just say we're friends. When you're ready to let a real man take care of you, adore and provide for you and be your Boaz, then I'll be more than prepared to elevate us from friendship to courtship. I would never play with your emotions or state falsehoods to you. I mean what I say. You're worth the wait."

She was blushing again and he chuckled, making her bright eyes snap into his.

"Are you laughing at me?" she frowned.

"I love it when you blush. It's the most beautiful, artistic work of art I've ever witnessed. I really get a kick out of it," he teased her as he playfully tapped the end of her nose.

Royale rolled her eyes, but she liked the playful banter and his attention. There was something special about Khan, something that made her forget her fears and feel free to trust again. There was no other way for her to explain it. She was completely smitten and captivated by his honesty and spirit. His ability to maintain his equanimity after she shared her concern about being in a relationship stunned her, but in a good way. He might just be what she needed to begin again. "Whatever. Now, tell me what caused you and your father to have such an epic blow up?" she questioned, and as soon as she did, his face transformed.

"I don't want to discuss it because it would ruin this perfect moment, but I'll say this. He and I just don't agree, and it's best that we go our separate ways before one of us hurts the other."

She frowned at his admission. There was definitely something going on, but she respected his need for privacy. If he wasn't ready to have a conversation about what had happened, she understood. She did leave Virginia to escape having to face the drama that seemed magnetic. "I won't pry. Believe me, I understand about wanting to avoid drama. How about you come inside, get a shower, then I can tell you about my drama?"

"What's going on now?" he asked, concerned.

She teasingly slapped his arm and did a dramatic eye roll before answering. "I'll tell you later. Now, you get a shower, and I'll fix you some breakfast. We'll talk, and maybe I'll help you at work today."

He smiled. "Sounds good."

♦ ♦ ♦

Royale sat down at the receptionist desk because Khan's secretary had called in sick and he needed her to assist him. She didn't mind, but she would have rather been with him and his crew since she had limited time in West Virginia. She wanted to spend as much time as she could with him. After kissing him, it was like a jar of butterflies had been released in her stomach and she felt like she was a teenager. In just a short time, Khan had brought life and brightness in her dull existence. She hadn't been depressed or angry since he helped her that night when she had nearly crashed her car.

While she was in Nairobi, all she thought about were her shortcomings, all the things she had done wrong or failed at that made Matan choose Royce over her. She over analyzed and scrutinized her entire body, fearing she was too fat and that he had lost interest. In worrying about that, she lost weight, a lot more than was probably healthy in such a short time. Then she wondered if her values were old fashion, and even though he wanted to be a pastor, maybe he wanted her to take their relationship to the next level, which she was going to do that night, but it had been too late.

Shaking the unhealthy thoughts, she placed her Surface Book on the desk and opened it up. Khan had told her to entertain herself. He might be longer than expected as he had some homes he needed to personally check on, as well as visit with his crew. All she had to do was answer the phone and take messages, and other than that, she'd be bored. Since the phone wasn't ringing and she was the only person in the office, she thought it was time to check her email. That was the only account she hadn't deactivated. Only her family, select church family and friends had knowledge of this private email address.

Now that Khan had boosted her confidence, she was ready to read whatever it was that Matan and her family had sent her. She connected to Khan's Wi-Fi, then clicked on the Google icon to check her Gmail account. She hadn't touched it in eight weeks, so she knew there had to be over one thousand emails. Taking a deep breath, she logged in and was surprised to see that she had an email from Matan dated last night.

Below were emails from her father, grandparents and more from Matan, plus church members, sorority sisters. Seeing Matan as the most recent email was shocking, only because she assumed after the scene he'd made in Starbucks, he wouldn't reach out. Apparently, she was incorrect in her assessment of his desperation to be heard. She wouldn't underestimate him again. She clicked the email, partly out of curiosity and partly out of closure. She needed to know where she had failed at being a girlfriend.

I'm sorry. I know you don't believe me, and it probably seems redundant due to all the previous emails I've sent. I apologize for the previous emails where I sound harsh, I just miss you. I miss you so much. I'm so very sorry for what you witnessed between your mother and me. I'm sorry about how I behaved at Starbucks. The last thing I ever wanted to do was hurt or embarrass you. I was in my feelings, missing you, and allowed my emotions to get the better of me. You didn't deserve that. If you allow me a second chance, I'll earn back your trust, love, and friendship. I can't live without you. I'm a better man when I'm with you. I know that now. I believe deep down, you have it in your heart to forgive my mistakes and sins. I need you to forgive me so I can forgive me. We both need to heal.

I want you to know that the relationship I had with your mother had nothing to do with you. I never want you to think you lack in any way. You're everything a man could want, wish or pray to have. I was just stupid. I fell for lies and lust. I was completely under her spell, and then when you caught us, it was like a splash of water on my face, an awakening of sorts. It was when I lost you that I realized just how much I needed you. Life has sucked these past few months, which led me to overreact at Starbucks. I'm in mourning because I've lost you, my mentor and father figure, and sadly, I've lost my path to God.

I feel so unworthy. As I write this email, I feel…I feel like I'm nothing, as if I don't deserve to breathe air or walk among the living. Just please come back home. I know how when you feel overloaded, you escape to think, but usually, all that happens is you stress yourself out more. If you aren't ready to talk to me, I understand, but don't shut your family out. Just in case you're wondering how I know you've left Virginia, I overheard Ma Gwendolyn talking to Sister Earline.

Fontaine and the guys are taking me on a trip to reset my mind, then hopefully, you and I can work on our relationship. My numbers are still the same for the landline and cell if you want to talk to me. I love you, Royale, and I always will. I'll wait for you until my last breath.

-Matan Graymond Haddon

It wasn't until tears rested on her forearm did, she realize she was crying, and that angered her. Matan wasn't worth her tears, or emotions of any sort. It annoyed her how he made it sound like he was a victim and like he needed her permission to forgive himself. She wouldn't fall for it, no matter what. Taking a cleansing breath, she wiped her tears and glanced up as she felt her personal space being invaded.

When she looked up, there stood a familiar woman. Although she couldn't recall her name, she did recognize the ginger hair. Royale knew she was one of the two women at the restaurant that she and her friends had visited. Pulling out a Kleenex to wipe her eyes and nose, she quickly got her appearance together and offered the scowling woman a smile.

"Good afternoon, how can I assist you today?" Royale asked in her most professional tone, hoping she covered up her emotional moment.

"Where's Judy, and why are you here?" Everleigh queried, agitated.

Hearing the attitude and seeing the pissy disgust that followed on her oval face, Royale's mind switched. *Not today, Satan. Don't bring that crap today*, she thought inwardly as she tilted her head to the side. The movement allowed her hair to cascade down her shoulder as she glared at the woman who looked like she was going on thirty. It was evident by her blotchy skin that she was getting an overload of vitamin D from the sun. Royale debated on offering her a referral to a dermatologist to fix that mishap. Instead, she refrained from insulting the woman and reached down deep in her sweet tank. God knows, she didn't have the patience she once had before her vessel and ex-boyfriend decided to have an affair. Her soul had taken a blow, and her armor of God wasn't fully on, so she was a ticking time bomb.

Royale cleared her throat before replying. "Well, Ms. Judy called and took a personal day. Since you seem acquainted with her, I'm sure you can phone her to get a more detailed response as to why she needed to take the day."

Royale eyed the feisty redhead and noted how her thin, wrinkled lips formed in an irritated *O* shape. Royale suspected it was because she couldn't believe that Royale would respond so smartly. Well, she was getting edified today.

The woman before her flicked her lengthy, wavy, garnet hair behind her feminine shoulders. Royale held her snicker when the woman epically failed at hiding her kaleidoscope of emotions. She was attempting to throw Royale off, but it didn't work. Her elementary actions were unsophisticated and easy to interpret. Ol' girl was really coming for her as she narrowed her malachite eyes, preparing to shoot daggers. Unfortunately, her flaming crimson cheeks indicated to Royale that she had hit her mark, and this girl was probably all bark and no bite. It wasn't that she was attempting to go tit for tat, but there was something about this woman that sent off warning bells and brought out her inner mean girl.

"Where is Khan? I need to see him." Without waiting for Royale to answer, she snapped, "You know what, I'll just see my way to his office. I wasted enough of my time with you."

Royale's eyes widened at the disrespect and nasty attitude. Gingersnap was asking for it, and Royale was about to adhere to her request. "No, ma'am, you won't. Khan isn't here, he's out with his work crews. What I can do is either take a message, assist you, or you can call his cellphone and discuss your business. I'm sure since you two are *friends*, you know his number."

This time, Royale must have hit the ultimate nerve because the woman went through a transformation right before her eyes. Then, she let out an unladylike snarl before leaning down and over the desk that Royale was sitting behind. She was right in Royale's face, so close, Royale was tempted to offer her some Altoids and a Listerine packet to freshen her breath. She must have eaten a burrito or something because boy, her breath was lit like the Olympic torch. Royale was forced to lean back a bit. There was no need for her to faint from the fire breath Gingersnap was exhaling. She was sure the antagonistic, asinine female thought she backed away because of fear, but that was far from true.

"Let me inform you of something. I know *your kind* think that because of Obama and discrimination laws, you can sass your white superiors, but I strongly suggest you dial it down. I won't tolerate inferior, welfare-recipient crack whores disrespecting me. Your time is ending!" she growled as the hate of her words spewed out. Then she whipped out her index finger like she was chastising a child, before continuing. "Please know that when I contact Khan, I'll be complaining about you. Just so you know, I'm not scared of *your kind*. I know you all respond well to masters, ropes, and whips, so next time, I'll bring my slave kit!" she sneered, winked and then walked away, leaving Royale asphyxiated by indignation.

It took Royale a moment to catch her breath and comprehend what had transpired. This woman, who she didn't know, had just gone ballistic with her racist assault. Never in her life had she ever been spoken to with such scornful antipathy. She was so enraged, she wanted to cry.

The inner Malcolm X with a mixture of Amanda "Lioness" Nunes in her wanted to go one hundred percent savage. She could visualize knocking her ginger hair the color of the Snow Queen Elsa and beating her blotchy skin to an even, white buttercream. However, she clamped down the violent rage, although the frustration and outrage were still present. She was so furious by the woman's aberrant behavior that her left leg bounced uncontrollably, and she continued to flex her fist open and closed as she tried to find her place of peace and pray.

Her prayer wasn't having its immediate effect because she couldn't calm herself enough to pray right. She was so offended, she started talking out loud to herself. Her mind was replaying how she should have responded, instead of sitting like a lump on a log. That woman had really tried it, and Royale had done nothing to defend herself. She had allowed that female to get the better of her, which was probably why her vessel had taken her man. Everyone assumed the bishop's daughter was a coward. Not even close. She just tried to be slow to anger, slow to speak and quick to listen. Today she wished she had been quick to anger, quick to speak and slow to listen. That racist hussy needed to be taken down a few notches.

After a good twenty minutes, Royale finally calmed down enough to pick up the telephone. She quickly dialed Kisha. She needed to talk this out so she didn't do something drastic and dangerous. The Bible clearly stated that vengeance is mine says the Lord, but she was feeling worldly and wanted to seek her own revenge.

"Hello?"

"Kisha, it's me. Girl, you won't believe what just happened. I'm stupid mad. You know that kind of mad that have you acting superhuman? Well, that's my state of mind."

"You've got to be mad to be using slang terminology. Tell me, you know I can't take the suspense. If Khan did something idiotic after all you've been through, then I'm kicking his butt."

"It wasn't Khan. Do you remember that ginger-haired, Amazon looking girl who was with the overweight blonde girl that night we all went out?"

"Yeah, Everleigh."

She snapped her fingers when Kisha said her name. "Everleigh, that's her name. Anyway, she came for me. She went off on some racist rant because Khan isn't in the office. You know what she called me? I quote, because as long as I live, I'll never forget those aspersive remarks. That *child of God*—I say that with dripping sarcasm—said, '*I won't tolerate inferior, welfare-recipient crack whores disrespecting me.*'" Then she followed up with, '*I know you all respond well to masters, ropes, and whips,*' all while pointing her index finger in my face. Girl, I wanted to show my tail and let her catch these hands, but all I did was sit in this chair looking like *boo boo the fool*. I wasn't prepared for that kind of verbal assault."

"What the...? Oh, my mercy, girl, I'm coming over there. I'll show her. She must think they're still casting for *Twelve Years A Slave*, coming at somebody like that. I never could stand that Oompa-Loompa, Raggedy Ann looking doxy.

"Where's Khan at? I know for a fact he doesn't get down like that. Ol' racist wench. She must not know how we get down. She's ignorant, but please believe I can be ignorant too. You know she's a member of that Christian Identity. That's a religion I don't understand. They're just another racist terrorist organization that needs to be eliminated. ISIL, IS or whatever they call them terrorist ain't got nothing on them white, right-wing extremist.

"I'm so ticked off! Fix it, Jesus, and fix my heart because saved souls don't think deadly thoughts. I swear I'll go straight Samson with a side of David on her Sodom and Gomorrah butt. Okay! She don't want to see that side of Nakisha Byse."

Even though Royale was upset, she had to laugh at Kisha's antics. Her friend was so upset, she was humming "Lift Every Voice and Sing". Yeah, she was in beast mode. "I'm so livid. I was already emotional after reading an email I received from Matan. I'm working on not triggering my anxiety, but that woman threw me for a loop. I have no idea where the animosity is coming from. I don't know her and she came at me with such bold contempt, you'd think I had taken Khan from her. Who does that?"

"A racist wench with a bad attitude, that's who. Look, I'm getting in my car now. I suspect you're in the office alone, and I don't think that's a good idea with the racist mafia on the loose. I know that all white people aren't that way, but sometimes...let me not go there. Just stay on the phone with me until I get there."

"I'm not scared of her, she just ticked me off. If she returns, I'll be ready! Please believe, she can catch these holy ghost hands. For real!"

"Girl, you sound too much like me. I'ma have to use that one, though. *Holy ghost hands*. A'ight, look, I know you aren't scared, but I feel better being there with you until Khan arrives."

"Fine." Just as she uttered the word, a white man entered. He was as tall as Khan, and just as wide. He looked like a real cowboy with his boots, wrangler jeans, belt buckle, button-up shirt and black cowboy hat. He was eye-catching, even had a cute nose like Tim McGraw, but instead of feeling welcoming and warming, she felt tense and uncomfortable.

She steadied her eyes on him, studying his body language, looking for threats, all while fishing in her purse for her stun gun. She wouldn't be caught off guard twice in one day. She really couldn't get away because she hadn't driven; she had ridden with Khan, so it was fight or die in her mind.

"Ma'am?"

"Who is that?" Kisha asked, concerned.

"I don't know," Royale replied, looking at the man, then back at her purse.

"Ask him," Kisha urged.

Royale rolled her eyes and let out a dramatic sigh, but did as Kisha requested. "Sir, how, um…how can I assist you?" she finally stuttered out, terrified, but hoping it didn't show. She finally had her stun gun in hand but kept it hidden from the man who was now standing in front of her desk.

"Well, you aren't Judy."

For some reason, that statement set her off. "Nope, and if you're going to attack me, I'll lay you out. Please believe I'm in savage mode and I have zero patience for any asinine antics. In laymen terms, I'll slay a Goliath today," she announced with bravery.

He seemed stunned at her aggressive statement, and quickly put his hands up in an act of submission, the side grin he had now completely gone. "Ma'am, just calm down. I'm Canton Knight, some call me CK. I'm Khan's cousin from Texas. I'm just looking for him. I mean you no harm, I swear," he replied, his Texas drawl thick and honeyed.

"Hold on," she told him, as she turned her attention back to Kisha. "Kisha, do you know a Canton Knight, he claims to be Khan's cousin."

"Oh yeah, CK is a sweetheart. Don't hurt that fineness. I can't believe you told that man you were in savage mode and would slay him like David did Goliath. Honey child, I officially just flatlined. You got over being scared with the quickness, though," she replied with humor in her voice.

Royale then looked back at Canton. His grin had returned after hearing Kisha verify his identity, and he was most likely laughing at the humor in Kisha's voice, who was mimicking her. Royale cleared her throat and looked Canton square in the eyes. "I'm sorry, Canton. It's just, a woman came in here earlier and verbally attacked me. She was on a racist tirade, and I honestly thought she had sent you to physically injure me."

"What?" His blue lava eyes widened at the accusation. "Ma'am, I would never. My mother would hem me up by my breeches. I've never hurt a woman. Who was this lady? Let me call Khan. Did she hurt you? Are you okay?"

He fired the questions so rapidly that she couldn't answer them all. His concern comforted her, and she nodded no to assuage his growing anxiety. "My pride is all that was hurt. I'm sorry about the way I greeted you. That was unprofessional. Let me start over. I'm Royale, and I'm just helping Khan out today because Judy called in and couldn't make it. I think I should've just routed the landline to his cell and rode around with him. That way, I could have avoided the Everleigh situation."

"Oh, you're Royale," he stated with a big grin, showcasing perfectly aligned Rembrandt teeth.

"Royale!" Kisha yelled.

"Huh?" she answered, realizing she was ogling the heck out of Khan's cousin. He really had the most entrancing set of cerulean eyes, and his bronze skin only made his eyes glow brighter. Now that she wasn't scared, she could observe him better. Canton Knight worked out and he was fineness. He had a nice build. He had a dimple like Khan, and he had lips like Chord Overstreet. He was gorgeous, with a thick mass of dark curls that he let loose when he removed his black cowboy hat. She bet he was a heartbreaker.

Kisha sucked her teeth, and Royale wondered if she knew she was checking Canton out. "I'm hanging up, but I'm still coming over. You're safe with Canton's fine self. He is a real gentleman."

"Okay, girl, talk to you when you get here." She hung up and turned her attention back to Canton. He had a sheepish smirk that was identical to Khan's. She couldn't help but smile at him.

"You sure are pretty. Khan said you were, but I didn't believe him. I tell'ya, the camera doesn't do you justice. I saw your show, and I liked it. Well, I like you and your cousin. You were the only two who seemed real," he flirted and then added, "How about I grab us some sodas from the break room and you can tell me all about this rude customer. Maybe I can offer some assistance. I'm a lawyer. I don't do Civil Rights Law, I do Oil and Gas Law, but I can be of help."

She let out a timid giggle, followed by a deep blush.

"Royale?"

"Hm?" She looked up at him with doe eyes.

"You gonna put that stun gun up? I ain't gonna hurt'cha, and I really don't want'cha to hurt me either," he stated, slipping from his professional speech to his southern twang.

"Sorry." She put it away and they both headed toward the break room and continued talking.

CHAPTER 10

Ronald removed the ice pack he had been using to nurse his bruised, swollen cheek to take a swallow of his beer. He hoped the beer would ease the throbbing he was currently suffering. He couldn't believe Khan had fought back, and then took all his clothes and left him on the bed, not knowing if he were dead or alive, but part of him was proud. He didn't know his son had it in him to be violent. The other part of him was enraged and vexed by his son's assault on him because he found fault with his beliefs and depiction of the inferior blacks. The boy was all backwards, and hadn't been right in his head since he had witnessed the murder of his momma. Even before that, Khloe had the boy sissified.

Shaking his head in dismay, he reached for his cellphone and dialed Hoss. He needed to get drunk tonight, and then he would decide how to handle his son. He had his priorities all mixed up and needed some guidance. He was really thinking about letting the boys get ahold of him and teach him a lesson he so badly wanted to learn.

"Yeah?"

"Hoss, it's Ronald. You got any plans later tonight?"

"Not really, thinking of going to Teagan's bar and drinking."

"Well, if you do, come and get me. The boy and I got into an altercation and he knocked me flat on my keister and left me for dead. I didn't know he had it in him. I just wish he understood that I'm not the enemy," Ronald complained. He just didn't know how to make Khan see the truth. Race mixing was wrong. Whites and blacks were never meant to be together, and Kalid Giles was proof that blacks were dangerous and uncivilized, yet his son continued to associate with them. He needed to find a way to stop him.

"What'chu talkin' 'bout? You said he done did what?"

"We came to blows, it got ugly and he left. Now I'm nursing a beer and icing my face."

"I'm coming over. You need to get that son of yours under control."

"I will, Hoss, I will."

♦ ♦ ♦

Khan sat in near apoplectic shock after hearing what Everleigh had said to Royale. *A slave kit?* That was overboard and insulting, to say the least. He didn't know what to say to soothe Royale. Honestly, he had hoped to keep that part of his life away from Royale. In time, he wanted to ease her into the information about his father and his beliefs, but this situation had just moved up the timeline.

Here he was, motionless on the outside, but on the inside, his body was chaotic. He was surrounded by Kisha, Nehemiah, Canton and Royale. Three of them knew his story as if they lived it, and only one was completely ignorant to the mess he called life. He could tell Royale was stuck between not being led by her anger and forgiving the trespass against her or seeking retribution for Everleigh's philistine philosophy. However, had he and Royale changed roles, God forgive him, but Everleigh would have been in the ER. Shaking his head, he finally attempted to participate in the conversation that was taking place.

"Royale, can we speak in my office?" he requested.

She shook her head in the affirmative and he got out of his chair and the pair walked away, leaving the others to socialize amongst themselves. He knew by the look Nehemiah had given him, that after he settled things with Royale, he and Nehemiah would have to have a conversation as well. The only good thing about the day was that he no longer lived in his father's house. After work, he and Canton were heading to Nehemiah's apartment. Nehemiah's father had just arrived a few hours ago, so Nehemiah could return to his own home, where Khan had a room.

Once they arrived in his office, he shut the door and motioned for Royale to take a seat. He let out a sigh when she did. Her illuminating copper eyes stared directly into his, and he got a brief insight into how injured her feelings were. He was barely able to hold her stare. He knew she'd been through enough with her family, the media, and now this. He wanted to be her haven, not her headache. Calming his thoughts, he walked up to her and squatted down as he reached for her hands and covered them with his own. The contrast between color and size made him smile. He adored her melanin. How could something so simple as melanin cause so much anger, hate, and death? How could anyone hate someone as beautiful as Royale?

"I apologize for what took place today. I had no idea that Everleigh would show up at the office. I mean, there was no reason for it. I have limited interaction with her. In fact, that night was the first time I had seen her after telling her I didn't want to pursue a relationship. She and I aren't friends on any level. However, she'll be hearing from me after what she said to you," he told her, as he did his best to maintain his lividness with the situation.

"You don't need to apologize for her behavior. However, I do have a question. The altercation between you and your father, did it stem from your interaction with me because I'm of African American descent and not of European descent?"

He averted his gaze. Today with her had started off great. They had shared a kiss, and he had finally told her how he felt. Right now, he feared that their budding relationship was at risk. Lord knows, he wasn't willing to lose this woman, not now, not ever. If that meant completely disowning his father, then so be it.

He was thinking about how to articulate himself without using too much verbiage when she removed one hand and rested it under his chin, causing him to be imprisoned by her eyes. He loved the color of her eyes. They were a usual honey-copper color that seemed to change into a lighter hue when she was worried. She always stole his breath away.

"Tell me, please."

Khan suspired in acquiescence. He had to tell her the truth and pray for the best. "Yes and no. My father had no idea I was out with you, just my black friends. He hasn't been the same since my mom was murdered by a black man. In his mind, all black people are evil and untrustworthy.

"His animus has fueled his hatred. He attempted to raise me in his image, to hate people who aren't white, but I never did. It never felt right. Long before my mother was murdered, Momma Byse had been in my life; she and my mother were friends. Nehemiah and I reconnected in high school when I persuaded my dad to stop homeschooling me.

"So, in his mind, I'm a failure for not spewing hate speech, and for not preaching white power and supremacy. This morning was the straw that broke the camel's back. Forgive the cliché, but it's the truth. He came at me violently, but he didn't hurt me because he's suffering from osteoarthritis, so his efforts were fruitless. I did hurt him, though. I knocked him out cold, threw him on his bed and left." He paused to see if Royale was negatively impacted by his act of violence, but she listened with a nonjudgmental expression and he continued. "I'm done, Royale. I can't live in that hate-filled trailer any longer," he confessed to her. He leaned his forehead to hers. No longer was he in a squatted position because his legs hurt, so he was now on his knees to ease the pressure. "Please tell me that what happened today with Everleigh and me telling you about my father won't make you view me differently. I don't want us to end before we begin."

"I do view you differently," she started.

"But—"

"Hold on, let me finish," she cut him off, her left hand now resting on his cheek. "I was saying I view you differently because it takes a strong individual to stand up to their only surviving parent. I can only imagine how it felt to lose your mother so violently. I'm sure the reason you stayed so long with your father was because he's all you have left, and I can't fault you for that. The hate your father believes in doesn't define you.

"I do admire you for standing against the injustice and ignorance that has surrounded you. I would never judge you or allow my feelings to be altered based on the actions of insignificant individuals like Everleigh. I'll not reevaluate our relationship based on the misguided assumptions and fallacies your father has made about an entire race of people based on the action of one." She sighed but continued. "I am, however, afraid. Not of Everleigh or your father, but I'm frightened because, for the first time since my vessel's and ex-boyfriend's perfidy, I feel a kindling in my heart. My mind tells me it's too soon to feel this way, but I can't deny it. I can't deny you.

"I like you, Khan. I want to get to know you better and explore where we can go, but I don't want you to feel like you need to hide or keep secrets from me. In fact, I implore you not to do that. It only causes agony and affliction. I've had enough of that. Please respect me enough to be honest with me, and I promise I won't make you regret it."

He wanted to tell her he loved her just for saying that. The feeling of relief that washed over him was so freeing. He had waited his entire life for this moment, for this woman who excited and impressed him daily. "I'm going to kiss you now. Your words just kissed my heart, and I need to physically share with you how you're making me feel right now."

"Khan Masterson," she playfully chastised.

He so loved how his name sounded on her lips. Her accent was a siren song that drew him in. He placed his extra-large hand behind her head and guided her lips to his. She either ate a lot of cinnamon and honey, or her lip balm was made of it because she tasted like honey and cinnamon again. It fit her because she was oh so sweet and addictive.

Just as he was about to deepen the kiss, a knock at his office door interrupted them. They both moaned in unison at the distraction.

"Khan, c'mon, cousin, we're starving out here. Besides, I wanna get to know Royale better," Canton teased.

Royale giggled. "I like your cousin. He told me Czarina and I were his favorites on *The First Ladies of DC*."

"I bet he did," he told her before turning his attention to his cousin, who had now opened the door. "We're coming, Canton, shut the door."

"Nope, because if I do, you two will start kissing again and I'm hungry. So, let's go."

Khan laughed, but got up and reached his hand out to Royale to help her out the chair. It wasn't necessary, but he wanted an excuse to touch her. "Let's go then."

◆ ◆ ◆

Matan, Fontaine and three of their frat brothers, Tataya, Charles, and Maurice had arrived in Las Vegas, Nevada It was probably the last place Matan needed to be, but here he was. It was two o'clock back home, but Nevada was three hours behind Virginia, so they had time to check into their hotel, eat and sightsee before checking out the nightlife.

Once they rented an SUV, they headed out to the Paris Las Vegas hotel. Matan sat on the passenger side, while Fontaine drove. They were all eager to see what Sin City had to offer. As they headed out, Matan's cellphone started ringing. He had his landline calls forwarded to his cellphone in hopes that Royale would read his email and reach out to him.

As soon as he looked down, he knew who it was. It was his father, Magnus. Unbeknownst to his mother, he'd reached out to his father a few years ago, and they were trying to build a relationship. He had yet to tell his father about the scandalous situation he currently found himself in. He figured his father was calling him because Matan hadn't put money on his books for the month. His father must have gotten an illegal phone.

"Hello?"

"Matan, boy, what're ya doing?"

"Huh?"

"Son, don't huh me. You think I don't get the outside news in here. It took some time, 'cause I was in solitary for a minute, but I hear you cheated on your girl wit' her momma. What kinda mess is that?"

"Dad, listen."

"No, you listen. God knows I wish I never got locked up trying to protect yo momma 'cause all she done did is ruin you. Answer me this, that money you was putting on my books, were you getting them funds from your girlfriend's momma?"

Matan looked over at Fontaine, but he was busy listening to Tye Tribbett, which was one of Royale's favorite gospel artists. Then he looked back at the other three, but they were sleeping, so no one was paying any attention to the conversation he was having with his father.

"Matan, you know I got limited time on this phone. Now, tell me the truth, is you a gigolo? Is you pimping out your body to cougars? Just keep it one hunnid wit' me."

"Man, nah. I just got caught up."

"Caught up? Boy, you was having a sexual relationship with a married woman twice your age, albeit a bad ole gal, but still. She the mother of your girl, and let me say, your girlfriend is a beautiful thickem. I don't know what'chu was thinking. Then you disrespected Grayling, who I happen to like. See, me and him done had several conversations 'bout'chu before you violated the man's trust. Now I bet'cha looking like a lost puppy. I should have never taken the fall for yo' momma."

"Dad, you need to ease up on my momma. Why do you keep saying you took the fall? What does that mean? Nobody forced you to do an armed robbery, rolling up in them folks' house like you were the National Guard."

"Hush up, 'cause yo' momma's boy tail don't know the entire truth, but I'll let Roslyn fill you in since she all saved and sanctified now. Listen here, why is you suing them people after all the pain you caused? You know good and well they ain't defamed your name. If anything, they should sue you."

Matan growled and rolled his eyes. His father couldn't see his dramatic animation, but that didn't stop him from being extra. Even when Fontaine looked at him as though he had lost his mind, he continued. "I'm curious how you even know about that, but I assure you, I'm not suing anyone. All I want to do is get my girl back and relocate to Boston to attend school. Momma is the one suing. Between you and me, I think she got it in for Royce. I told her to drop it, but she's determined."

"Firstly, don't be growling at me with'cha nasty self. I'm still your father. Secondly, you need to man up and apologize to Royale and Grayling. Additionally, young buck, you need to stay away from Royce. That woman is just as dangerous as your mother. They got an old-school rival that dates to high school."

"I figured. Look, Dad, I can't talk freely, but when I get back into town, I will come see you, and we can talk."

"All right, and send me some more of them Bible studies. They help me. Oh, and did I tell you they moved me into a new cell with a new cellie? I like this dude. His name is Kalid. He helping me get into one of the college programs."

"Good. I'm proud of you."

"Well, I gotta go."

"Okay, I'll see you next weekend."

"Cool. Bye." His father hung up.

♦ ♦ ♦

Royce looked at her parents, Patty and Eli. It was their turn to hear her grovel. She was still a little irritated that Matan hadn't come to see her or returned her phone call. He owed her that much. Like, she deserved at least a returned phone call, but then again, his Peppermint Patty momma, Roslyn, probably had him held so tight, he couldn't do anything. That woman got on her last nerve. She was sure Roslyn was probably all up in her husband's face, trying to rekindle what had no embers.

"Ro, are you going to say something, or should I start?" Patty asked.

"Sorry, mother, my mind has been scattered lately. When Gray was here, he told me our daughter had run off. I know she's an adult, but I worry about her. She's so sensitive, and I just don't want someone to take advantage of her diffidence."

"Well, now, that is an interesting statement. It would seem to me that's exactly what you did," Patty retorted.

"Mother!" she snapped in an admonishing tone. Her dark eyes pleaded with her mother to ease up in front of their mixed company. She could understand her mother's feelings toward the situation because of her standing in the public eye as well as the church, but there was no need to attack her in that way.

"No, don't 'mother' me. You were wrong. Ain't nobody raised you to act like that. Your selfish actions have destroyed this family. You got us looking like a bunch of heathens, and with your daughter's soon-to-be fiancé at that. What were you thinking?"

"Okay, everyone, just calm down," Janice interjected. "You aren't here to belittle each other. Royce needs your understanding and assistance; she doesn't need to be stressed. She's just as hurt as you all are. Can we please refrain from name calling and pointing fingers and try to find healing?"

Royce wanted to warn Janice because she didn't know about Patty Royce. She didn't take too kindly to being interrupted, nor did she like being told by a stranger how to act. Royce appreciated Janice attempting to come to her rescue. It seemed like no one was in her corner at the moment, and she needed some backup.

"Ms. Janice, I'm her mother, so kindly sit yourself back down and let me handle my daughter. I've been doing it since 1967, thank you very much."

Royce wasn't even stunned by her mother being so extra. That was typical Patty. Still, it was embarrassing, and she turned to her father for assistance. Surely, he would make her mother mind. "Daddy, are you going to allow her to speak to me that way? This process is about healing, not accusing. She is unjustly and unfairly attacking my character."

"Your mother is right, honey. Grayling said that Matan wasn't your only infidelity. He said you've been unfaithful for the last decade. Now, I'm not judging or condemning you, I'm just trying to ascertain what led you to this."

She shook her head, annoyed, and collapsed her head into her hand. She wanted to end this. She couldn't manipulate her mother like she did others. It bothered her that her mother was blaming her. Like, who cares what other people think? Why did Grayling tell her parents what she had told him? She let out a growl before replying. "Fine. As I told my husband, I was lonely. He was always out working and forgot about me, so I found emotional comfort in other men."

"How did you end up in bed with Royale's boyfriend? That's the part I can't wrap my head around. You have a good husband who has provided well for you, and a daughter any mother would love to have. How could you? Especially, when you claimed you didn't even like him for Royale because of the past you had with his mother. That's a separate conversation that needs to be had. Then you have an affair with him? I don't get that," Patty asked.

She didn't have to get it. She rolled her eyes as she quickly tired of her mother's overly dramatic antics. "It just happened, momma."

"For a year? It just happened for a year? Girl, you're lying. I know it, God knows it, and you know it. You're the worst kind of messy woman. I can't sit here while you play innocent. You got to be the worst representation of a first lady I've ever seen. I'm done. Talk to me when you are ready to take responsibility. Excuse me," Patty retorted and mumbled inaudible words as she departed.

Royce watched, stunned. It was unbelievable how Patty had flipped on her. She was prepared for the disappointment, but not the ire and accusations that followed. Her mother was extra, but this here was over the top and surprising. Then again, she shouldn't be surprised because her parents favored their only granddaughter, but she mattered too. Even though she wasn't a Rhodes Scholar, dean's list student, or in the process of creating her own nonprofit, she was still their child. All they ever did was praise Royale's accomplishments, and it angered her beyond belief.

Her mother slammed the door, leaving Royce, her father and a perplexed Janice sitting in silence. "Daddy, you need to talk to her. That immature display was inconsiderate and hurtful to my recovery. I'm the one in therapy, and I don't need the added stress. I've owned the fact that I made a mistake, but my goodness, I don't need to be punished and judged all over again," she pleaded with her father.

"Royce, my granddaughter is in West Virginia. I had to get a private investigator to find her just to ensure her safety because we all know who lives in West Virginia. Royale is coming back Sunday, so I suggest you work it out with your daughter. Now, this entire ordeal has upset your mother, and that effort would go a long way with your her. I love you, sweetheart. I want you to make a full recovery, get your faith back on track and your family. Please make the most of this opportunity. I'll come see you later."

She nodded as tears fell softly down her cheek. "I understand, and I love you. Thank you, daddy," she replied, reaching out to hug him before he left. He said the same and the two parted.

Once he was gone, she looked at Janice and let out an exasperated sigh. This was hard, confronting her family and apologizing for her behavior. She didn't like how she felt after speaking with her parents. Nothing had been resolved, and that was the point of this exercise. She still had to face Gwendolyn, Czarina, Matan and Royale. Her daughter would be the worse.

"Royce, what are you thinking?" Janice asked.

"That my daughter had the right idea. I should've just run far from here. I should've left it all behind. Lord knows I had enough men begging me to leave Grayling for them."

"It'll work out, but you have to go through the process and be honest, Royce. It's always best to go with the truth because lies always hurt worse."

That was only true if the lies were found out. Right now, she was Team Lie-and-keep-the-truth-to-herself. What had just happened only made her feel worse. If they knew the secrets she was carrying, her husband would divorce her, and her parents would disown her. Right now, her lies were keeping her safe.

CHAPTER 11

Royale was floating on cloud nine as she entered the bedroom she used while staying with the Byses. She only had two more days, then she would go back to Virginia. She flopped on the bed and pulled out her Surface Book. She wanted to Skype Khan, as if they hadn't just spent hours together, but honestly, she couldn't get enough of him. It was like they'd known each other for a lifetime.

When her computer awoke from its sleep setting, she noticed she had an incoming call. It was Ma Gwendolyn.

"Hey, Ma. How are you?"

"I'm better now that I can see you. Are you still coming home Sunday?"

"Yes, ma'am. As soon as church dismisses, I'll head to your house. However, I won't be there long because school starts soon and I have to get myself situated."

Royale saw the deepening frown on Gwendolyn's face.

"Well, honey, you're attending graduate school in Washington DC, and I prefer you just commute. So, everything should be fine. Besides, I want you to see someone about these anxiety attacks."

She knew for a fact the family assumed she was staying local, but she was going out of state. In fact, she had a great financial aid package to attend the University of Pennsylvania. "Actually, I've elected to attend school out of state."

"Why, Royale? Is this because of the incident with your father? He made a mistake, honey. He won't do it again."

"It isn't that, I just need a new start. I can't do that in Virginia. You have my word that I'll be there Sunday night, and I haven't had any anxiety attacks. They were mild anyway, nothing that needs attention."

"Well, I want a professional opinion about that. We'll discuss this again."

"Ma Gwendolyn, I'm about to turn twenty-four. I mean this in the most respectful way possible, but I don't require permission from you or my dad. I love you, and I respect your opinion, but in the end, the decision is mine alone."

"Well, I guess all I can do is accept that. Good night, sweetheart. I love you, and please forgive your father and talk to him. He's going through it, worrying himself sick after finding out you had an anxiety attack that caused you to nearly have a car accident. I was coming to get you myself, but I have no idea where you are."

"I'm in West Virginia at my soror Kisha's house."

"What part of West Virginia?" she questioned, concerned.

"Charleston. I'm not near him, so don't worry."

"Well, we'll talk tomorrow. I'll let you go, but promise me when you get home, you'll see your father. He's suffering, too, and you both need each other. I want this to be the last time you run and ignore your family. I know you received all of our emails."

"Yes, ma'am, and I apologize. I'll talk to Daddy when I get back home."

"Splendid, my dear. Good night for real this time."

"Good night."

♦ ♦ ♦

Khan was grinning like the Cheshire cat after getting off the phone with Royale. She'd told him she was going to Virginia to settle things with her family, and then she was heading out to Philly, and he told her he was going to Philly with her. She just brought out his protective nature.

"Dang, you're smiling hard," Canton teased.

"What can I say, my Honey Drop has that effect on me."

"Wait. Is Honey Drop Royale?" Nehemiah asked, confused.

"Yes. It's my pet name for her."

"Whoa, y'all moving fast like that? You think that's wise? I thought we discussed that you two were better off as friends, considering your and her situation," Nehemiah reminded.

"Ne, I can't help how I feel about her. She and I talked, and she's cool with it."

"She's cool with your dad being affiliated with hate groups?" he questioned incredulously.

"Well, I told her about his racist beliefs."

"But, bruh, that isn't the same as telling her your father is associated with an organization that murders people. I'm still trying to understand why they haven't put a hit on Kalid for what he did to your mother unless he got some kind of hookup we don't know about. Your dad is a retired police officer, so you know he has connections in the prison system."

"He has a legitimate concern, Khan. Plus, with the racist climate elevating and all these videotapes of cops killing African Americans—"

"I mean, she needs to know," Canton cut in.

"Why? I'm done with my dad, and I'm not in any way affiliated with any of his racist organizations. The only thing I'm keeping is my last name. He no longer exists to me. I choose Royale. I want to be with her, and I want to leave the drama behind."

"I'm concerned. Your dad won't let you go that easily. Just because you put it behind you, doesn't mean he put it behind him. I think he's going to retaliate, and we shouldn't underestimate the desperation of wounded pride and arrogant stupidity. It isn't over," Nehemiah stated.

Khan shook his head. Why did Nehemiah have to be so dire and negative? "Well, you might be right, but Royale won't be here. Let's table that for a moment, I got something else to tell you both."

"What?" they asked in unison.

"I got a letter from Kalid Giles, and he wants me to visit him. He claims he is innocent. There had to be something to it because the Innocence Project. It's a nonprofit legal organization that assists clients who have been wrongly convicted by DNA testing, has picked up his case. I think the DA in the case may have withheld evidence or something because of my dad being a cop."

"What? Are you going to see him?" Canton asked.

"Originally, I was going tomorrow, but I have decided to postpone until next week. I'd rather take Royale hiking. I want to make as many good memories as I can with her. I know once I meet up with Kalid, things will get real. I suspect there is more to my mother's murder than what I have been led to believe. That's heavy, and I can't do heavy right now."

"Dude, are you purposely trying to get your dad to hurt you?" Nehemiah questioned, concerned.

"No. Ne, you're giving a disabled old man way too much power. He doesn't have that type of power or connection, and he has no idea who Royale is."

"Dude, you're not giving him enough. Besides, Royale is famous, her family is wealthy, and she's all over the freaking media. He will know soon enough, and he will act out badly."

Khan was about to respond but could tell by Nehemiah's face that he was on a roll, so he let his friend finish his thoughts. He was definitely in preacher mode and couldn't be stopped even if he wanted.

"Now, come over here, we need to pray. The Bible says to pray about everything. Check out Philippians 4:6-7 after I lead us in prayer. A man who makes decisions without God's guidance is a fool. I have my reservations, Khan, but I can see you're really into Royale and won't listen to reason, so let's pray the hate away," Nehemiah lectured before bowing his head and extending his arms.

That was what Khan admired about Nehemiah Byse and his family, they had an unshakeable faith, and it had to be their prayers that had kept him when his mother was murdered.

♦ ♦ ♦

Early Saturday morning, Royale and Khan were heading to Overlook Rock Trail. She made sure that Khan knew she was a walker and not a hiker. There was no need for her to embarrass herself in his presence. However, she was excited about them spending alone time together. Since she had arrived, well, since they had met, the two of them had always been with a group so this would be an interesting interaction. Additionally, she wanted to discuss their future but didn't want to reach so deeply that her inquiries would scare him off. She sighed. She hated being in between. She needed that reassurance that he would be around once she started school.

Ever since things had ended with Matan, she second-guessed and doubted herself because of how she misread her relationship with her ex. Was she moving too fast and allowing her emotions to lead her? Was Khan a rebound? He surely didn't feel that way, and he told her before that wasn't the case, but in the back of her mind, she was still concerned. Men did lie. Yet, she wasn't convinced that she could trust her own judgment. She really needed to get back to God and let Him lead, then the confusion she felt wouldn't be there.

"What's on your mind?" Khan asked her as he made the turn at the light.

She bit her bottom lip, mulling over what she wanted to say and how best to present it without sounding like a nag or a stalker. Even in her inexperience, she knew men didn't like that. It was sad how one incident could completely alter one's self-assurance, perception, and confidence in themselves. Never had she been an insecure person, but now, it was almost the theme song of her life.

"Honey Drop?" he cooed, which caused her to laugh. She just couldn't get over the endearment. It sounded like a stripper name, but she did like the fact that he had deemed her worthy of a pet name.

"I've told you about that Honey Drop," she teasingly scolded. Her narrowed, copper, sunlit eyes held his, and a smile spread across his chiseled face.

"It makes you laugh, and I love the sound of your laughter. It's contagious. Seriously, you've been in deep contemplation since I picked you up. Are you nervous about it just being the two of us?"

She shook her head no. "That's not it. I felt comfortable with you that night you fixed my tire."

"I'm glad to hear that. Still, though, I know something has your attention. You're biting your lower lip."

She sucked her teeth at how observant he was. Then again, he was a landscaper, so paying attention to details was extremely important. "I was thinking about Sunday when I head back to Virginia, and um…we've had a good time, at least I have getting to know you and, um…"

"You're wondering when you go back to Virginia if what we have here in our little West Virginia bubble will burst. You're wondering if I'll change my mind about my feelings when you change your location. I was thinking the same thing about you. Let me calm any concerns you may have. It won't. If you want me to come to Virginia, I will. I'll help you move to Philadelphia too. I meant what I said, Royale. If me leaving my pop's house isn't enough to show you I'm serious about you and committed to seeing where this relationship can go, then tell me what I need to do to prove to you that this is real?"

When he looked at her like that, like she was this rare jewel, it made her body quake. She knew by the firmness of his jaw that he was genuine. "I…it's just that, oh see—"

"Take your time, it's just me you're talking to, no need to be nervous," he comforted as he placed his right hand over her clasped hands she held rested between her legs.

She nodded, feeling a calmness come over her. "It just that after what I witnessed between my vessel and Matan, it has made me a little self-conscious. Where I once didn't need validation or feel even an ounce of insecurity, I feel it now. I know that with your dad not approving of interracial relationships, even on a friendship level, I may lose you too," she confessed and then felt like a complete fool. She quickly dropped her head, wanting to run, but she was in his truck, so there wasn't anywhere to retreat. There she was, allowing herself to be vulnerable with a man she'd only known for less than a week. Her heart was so hungry for attention and needy for acceptance that maybe she was not thinking clearly.

"Hey, a queen doesn't drop her head. She might get down, but she never drops her crown. No man or situation is worth you dropping your head, ever," he told her as he placed his finger under her chin and lifted her head up. "Don't you ever feel ashamed about telling me how you feel. With me, I don't ever want you feeling insecure. I'm not Matan. My dad isn't an issue. I understand how what happened between your mom and your ex-boyfriend has had a negative impact on you. However, I believe once you get back to Virginia and settle things with them, you'll be able to move on. I'll be with you every step of the way."

Royale smiled at him and nodded in agreement. It was so nice to have someone be fully on her side. The way he comforted and connected with her made her think there was hope for happiness again. "I'm guessing that spiel about a queen and her crown is something you got from Nehemiah," she teased in an attempt to make light of a heavy conversation.

"Nah, he got it from me," Khan joked.

She laughed at him. Royale was completely in awe of how just eight and a half weeks ago, she was borderline insane with depression, her heart was broken, and her relationship and faith in Christ had been hanging by a thread. Then she met this man, who knew her from no one and had become her hero, and without even trying, had helped her get back to the woman she used to be.

With a smile, she sandwiched his hand between her smaller ones and leaned her head back in content. She let out a gratified breath, then nestled herself in the compatible silence until they arrived at the trail. She could tell right away that this place meant something to him. He was as giddy as a child in a candy store with unlimited funds. This made him happy, and she knew there was a story behind it, and she couldn't wait to hear it.

As soon as they exited the car, Khan grabbed both their backpacks, showcasing his massive, tanned arms. Today he wore a cutoff muscle shirt, a pair of shorts and hiking boots. She had on a long sleeve shirt, loose-fitting gray joggers and tennis shoes. He told her to be comfortable.

"Honey Drop, what exactly did you pack in your backpack?"

"Oh, well, I have some water, snacks, bug spray, SPF 30 sunblock lotion, chapstick, a First-Aid kit and a change of clothing," she told him and laughed at the look he gave her. "Lead the way, Khan. I'm excited to see this because you're so ecstatic about it."

"It's not even that long a walk and you brought everything and the kitchen sink," he joked.

"I just believe in being prepared."

She watched him chuckle, but she knew he was impressed by her preparation. She knew nothing about hiking or walking a trail, but she didn't want to get caught not having the essentials.

Khan waved her to come on and grabbed her hand and led the way. The two didn't talk a lot at first, and there were others out doing the same thing as them. It wasn't overly crowded, mostly moderate foot traffic. Royale listened as Khan told her about the area. Overlook Rock Trail was approximately a mile and a half, and Khan told her it was where the most beautiful wildflowers grew. The trail also offered numerous activities, and it was open all year round.

"Khan, the walking up wasn't so bad, but walking down has me a bit flushed."

"I got'cha. Do you need a break?"

"If you don't mind. I could use a sip of water."

The pair walked off the trail, and there was a large rock that they walked to and sat down. Royale thought the area was picturesque and took out her iPhone to take some pictures, and before she knew it, she was taking selfies of herself and Khan. He was such a good sport about it. He was really in his element, and she liked that.

After joking around a bit, Royale noticed how calm Khan had become. It was like he'd recalled a memory, and being the shutterbug, she was captured a few more photos of him using her iPhone. They were beautiful. If he ever wanted to pursue a career in modeling, he could. It was his long, thick mane that cascaded in the wind like a flag that caught her attention.

Then there was his muscled back. The man looked sculpted by the hands of God, and she was mesmerized by him. Even though there was so much she didn't know about him, she felt like she knew everything by the look in his eyes. She could observe him all day and never get bored. It wasn't just his physical beauty; it was the beauty that eyes couldn't see.

"Royale, come over here," he called to her, almost as if he had just remembered she was there.

She padded over to him and he pulled her down into his lap and her head naturally rested on his chest. She closed her eyes and inhaled his scent of Applewood, spice and a hint of aftershave. It made her insides tingle, and for a moment, she forgot what she wanted to ask him. He smelled so good. "Tell me what you were thinking."

He chuckled. "I was just remembering my mom and better times. I miss her. She loved the outdoors, and we came here a lot, but also to other parks, especially in Canada. This is where she came to get grounded. She said she liked to talk to God here." She felt him as his shoulders shrugged, causing her to look up at him. She could see that his blue orbs were floating in unfallen tears. His tanned skin was dressed crimson as he bit down on his bottom lip to hold in his emotions.

"I let her die, Royale. I let my mother die." His body shivered at the confession. Then the tears fell, and she wiped each one before turning fully around and embracing him. When she pulled back, she propped herself on his thighs and cupped his face.

"That's not true. You told me someone murdered her, and that isn't your fault."

"I was there, Royale. I was there, and I didn't save her. I didn't yell, I didn't fight, I just...I can't even remember what happened or what I did. Now the man who was convicted of killing her has reached out to me. He claims to be innocent, but I don't know. He might be—he must be since they're granting him a new trial.

"I know I don't feel the hate toward him my father does, but I've been having flashbacks. The thing is, I don't know if what I am remembering is fact or fiction. It's all a scrambling puzzle with no connecting pieces." He let out a deep breath before continuing. "I've been strong and tough all my life, Royale, but all my defenses fail when I'm around you. I feel again."

She smiled and kissed the tip of his nose that was now crimson, matching his cheeks. She leaned her head in for their foreheads to touch. "I'm here for you, Khan. Whatever you need, just ask, and if it's in my power to make it happen for you, then I will. If you want to see this man, then I'll go with you. You aren't alone in this. Even if we don't move beyond friendship, I'll be here for you."

"You're special, Royale," he said.

"You are too. Can I pray for you?"

"Right here? Like, right now?"

"Yes."

"Okay."

They bowed their heads and interlaced their hands and Royale began to pray.

♦ ♦ ♦

Khan felt his spirit lift as Royale prayed for him. It was like the barrier on his soul had been lifted and removed. When he had invited Royale to come on the trail, he had no intentions of getting emotional. He had buried the past and pain so deep inside, he pretended it wasn't there. It was easy to do because his father was continuously subjecting him to physical and verbal abuse. In order to survive, he'd learned not to feel.

Then Royale entered his life, and in just a few days, she became his guiding light. She had so many characteristics of his deceased mother it left him in awe. Her heart was good, she was sincere and thoughtful. Royale's greatest asset was her honesty. He knew it took a lot for her to share her feelings with him. Maybe that was why he felt comfortable breaking down in front of her, and he didn't regret showing his emotional side to Royale. She hadn't judged him. In fact, it seemed that it drew them closer together.

They were now walking hand in hand back to the truck, and his stomach had started growling, which caused Royale to laugh at him.

"I'm guessing you're hungry?"

"I can eat."

He chuckled as he opened the door for her to get inside. As they headed to get something to eat, Royale started talking about her hunting skills, how she liked going four wheeling and that one of her favorite reality shows was *Duck Dynasty*.

"Honey Drop, you might just be a redneck," he teased.

"Why?"

"You used to clog, you like *Duck Dynasty*, you hunt, go four wheeling, and listen to country music. Babe, that's rednecking it." That made her giggle, and he had to laugh as well. She simply amazed him and continued to surprise him. "So, Kisha was telling me something about you wanting to open an international nonprofit."

"Oh, well, it's in the works. I'm calling it Far Above Rubies. I've always done Christian missions, but when I was in high school, I went to Mali and discovered child brides, and it broke my heart. It became my passion. I found out the reason parents usually marry their daughters off young is because of political and/or financial reasons. It's a vast issue in developing countries, in parts of Asia, Latin America, Africa and Oceania.

"I've been to Niger, Chad, Bangladesh, Guinea, Central African Republic, and Ethiopia to educate families on why they should refrain from marrying their daughters off so young, and how keeping them in school can better help the family. Once you speak to the parents, they understand better. My organization will keep girls in school by offering them skills they can use to improve their communities and help their families. It's my hope by doing that, I can help decrease the cases of AIDS, empower and educate more women so they can help their countries, and help eliminate cases of obstetric fistula."

He noticed how serious she was when she spoke of her passion and it only deepened his feelings for her. He had no idea how one woman could be so full of love and compassion for others, especially after what her mother and ex-boyfriend had done to her. She truly was love and sincerely cared about others. That attracted him to her even more. "What is obstetric fistula?"

"Basically, obstetric fistula is a hole between a woman's vagina and one or more of her internal organs. Usually, when it happens in the villages, the young brides are shunned from their homes. After witnessing that, I knew I had to do something. God put us all in the world to be stewards and to utilize our gifts, and that's where He has led me."

"You're amazing."

"Not really, but I'm glad you asked me about it. It helps to put my issues in perspective. I need to focus on what I can change and not what I can't."

He reached over and placed his hand on her thigh and patted it lightly. "I'm sorry about what happened to you, but I thank God that He brought you to me. You're my breath of fresh air, and the goodness of your heart is like ointment to my soul. You're a treasure, Royale, and you have my word that's how I'll always treat you."

He felt her place her hand on top of his, and he smiled. He had just found his forever.

CHAPTER 12

Grayling entered the room where he was the last time, he met his wife. He'd been spending his time in prayer and meditation to calm his raging mind and to shield the fiery darts that Satan was attacking him with. Never in his life had he felt so confused, alone and scared. He truly feared the state of his family. Even after praying, he was extremely irritated and disappointed in his wife and himself. He should have known she was up to something, and he should have been prepared for the aftermath of vultures like Marc, but he wasn't. He had yet to get into contact with Marc, but his instinct told him his wife had to be involved, and if she were, he needed to stop her. Of course, it didn't help that he hadn't slept soundly since the departure of his daughter. There was a scripture in the Bible for every issue in life, yet he couldn't think of one. His faith was being tested, and he was failing.

Royale wasn't talking to him via Skype or email, but at least he knew her location, and she had assured his sister she was coming home Sunday night. That knowledge kept him somewhat composed, but he really wanted to go and get her. He just hoped Strom wouldn't reach out to her because that would upgrade the situation to critical. They didn't need to add that to an already hazardous situation that was impacting his family and church flock.

Clearing his mind, he sat down on the leather chair, bringing his hands together to form a temple. He closed his eyes and whispered a quick prayer to ease his mounting anxiety and beating heart. That was how upset he was, and he knew coming off that way wasn't good for either himself or his wife when she arrived. He didn't want his emotions to lead.

Inhaling deeply, her scent attacked him somehow. He hadn't heard the click of the door opening. Still, he kept his eyes closed. Surprisingly, he could recall a time when they were happy and in love, and those long talks they had about bringing God to the masses. A moment in time when she was his helpmate, his soul, the sun during a cloudy day. Once upon a time, she electrified his entire being. The sound of her voice could turn him from a solid to a liquid. How he adored her cute, little, dimpled chin that fit the tip of his thumb perfectly. There was a time when she was everything that was moral and virtuous. Now, her behavior, beliefs, and actions were anything but virtuous.

"Gray?" She called out to him, and he could hear the unsureness in her melodic voice. He knew why she was insecure. He had his eyes closed, and his face was unreadable. She had no way of being able to read him, and it made her unbalanced. Although that wasn't his intention, he was simply attempting to compose himself once more before accusing her of working with Marc to make more money off their predicament she'd created. He loved his wife, but he didn't love what fame had turned her into, and he wondered how much of him was to blame or had she been this way all along. Had he been blindsided by the beauty and the booty all this time? He didn't think so, but then again, he didn't know for certain.

"Yes, Royce?" His voice came off softer than he had anticipated.

"What's going on? Is Royale okay?"

For some reason, her concern for Royale seemed insincere to his ears, almost hostile. However, he answered her in a monotone voice. "As far as I know. She is scheduled to return home Sunday, but that's not what I came here to discuss. Please sit," he commanded as his dark eyes flickered open. He looked at her and watched as she sat down, and her shadow, Janice, took her seat in the corner of the room. He hoped she would remain silent because he didn't need her input today.

Grayling leaned forward, continuing to increase the tension. His eyes never left Royce and he slowly took in a mental inventory. She looked different, not unwell or sickly, but without her expensive clothes, makeup or some elaborate hairstyle, she seemed like the woman he knew. This, to him, was when she was her most beautiful. She was unhidden and possibly vulnerable. Maybe just maybe she would come clean, confess all her sins, repent and then they could move forward in their marriage. For him, divorce was the last recourse, but if that were the only way to resolve the issues, save his daughter and his church, then he would do it. He meant what he said; he would not lose his daughter to gain his wife.

"Royce, I'm going to ask you something, and I want you to be honest. For far too long, you've kept secrets from me, and I don't want that. Do you understand?"

"Yes, but what is this about?"

He let out an overdue sigh before answering her. "Marc reached out to Rina and pitched an idea about doing a reality show based on the girls. I guess kind of like *19 Kids and Counting* when the family went through that scandal, then the daughters reprised their roles with the new show. Well, I want to know if you had anything to do with it," he questioned, as he watched a myriad of emotions flash through her face before she answered him.

"It was just hypothetical."

Grayling nodded and shifted himself to relieve the tension in his body. "Really? Because before he approached Rina, he phoned me and asked me about doing a reality show based on our current situation. I declined. Let me make this crystal clear. The girls and I aren't doing any reality television. I don't believe you when you say it was just conjecture because he reached out to Strom. How does he know about him when none of us speak his name?"

Royce was shifting in her seat, her eyes no longer on his. Still, he maintained a calm demeanor, even after a good five tedious minutes had passed before she opened her mouth. Something changed in her mood that caused him pause. He leaned back in his seat and prepared for what was about to unfold. When his wife felt like she was being pushed into a corner, she turned straight honey banger.

"He's changed."

Grayling tipped his head to the side unsure if he'd heard her correctly. There was no way his wife was that doltish. She knew reaching out to Strom would and could split the family. Strom was truly a devil in disguise.

He had a vice grip on the armchair and glared at her, hoping he'd misconstrued what he'd heard. He could already feel his blood pressure rising. "Come again?"

Grayling watched her sigh, then looked at her counselor, he assumed for reassurance, which was strange to him. He waited patiently until their brief encounter ended and his wife turned her attention back to him.

"Strom has changed. Before all of this happened, he reached out to me. He wanted to know how his family was doing. Being the woman of God I am, of course, I sought to assist him in his spiritual journey. He wants to be in Czarina's life again, as her father. It's time we forgive him for his sins. Are we not all simply rags before God?"

He stilled. His body was as stiff as a corpse in rigor mortis when she made that confession. Strom had no right to ask about Gwendolyn or Czarina. He had forfeited that when they discovered he was an abusive bigamist. How dare his wife reach out to that man. "I'm her father!" Grayling bellowed, causing the counselor to jump in her seat and his wife to narrow her sable eyes while simultaneously sucking her teeth. She was in rare form tonight. Well, he was, too, so game, set, ready!

"You're her uncle! That nerves me so bad. I can't stand that you have your niece refer to you as Dad, and our daughter refers to your sister as Ma. I'm Royale's mother, and Royale is your only daughter. It's just wrong of you to try and replace her father."

The room went silent. It was all slow motion, the anger Grayling tried to rein in—boiling. Who was Royce to tell him how to treat his niece? This wasn't even the conversation he'd come to have. Lord knows, he had no idea she was in contact with Strom. There was no reason for the two to even be in contact. Her confession that she had been conversing with Strom had just changed everything. He could forgive the infidelity, but this, this was too much. He wasn't sure they could reconcile after this. Then it hit him, heavy and hard like a heart attack. Royce was probably having an affair with Strom too. It wasn't a farfetched conclusion.

"Were you sleeping with him too? Did you have an affair sexually or emotionally with that man?" he interrogated angrily. Grayling's nostrils flaring as he stood up and embedded his hands into his narrowed waist. He could see Janice trying to read the situation, wondering if she should intervene or call security. For her sake, she better stay seated and quiet because this didn't require her expertise.

"No, but you know what I've been wondering? What is going on between you and Gwen? It's mighty strange to me that after her husband left, you slid into the role of man in her life and her daughter's life. Strom suggested you two had an unusual relationship," she countered.

"How dare you suggest that I would have an incestual relationship with my sister. That's what you were implying when you used the term 'unusual relationship'. You're really repeating to me what that man said. That man, who is a bigamist, who lived a double life and nearly killed my sister and daughters. You have hit an all-time new low, which is difficult to do, considering you had sex with our daughter's boyfriend. You're a savage human being, selfish, rude and inconsiderate to allege that Gwendolyn and I would do something so disgusting and ungodly when you're the one who can't control yourself. How dare you call yourself a woman of God, woman thou aren't loose, and I have no time for it."

"Me? What about you telling my parents what we discussed? My mother went off on me and left. She looked at me as if I were nothing and called me a liar. That felt horrible, and you know what. It's just as much Gwen's fault as it is yours that I was forced to seek comfort in the hands of another because you placed her needs before mine. How dare you throw judgment against me, when I am what you created."

Grayling balled his hands into a fist to restrain from slapping some sense into his wife. He couldn't believe what she was saying. Was she on some revenge type drama? Was she so caught up in her sin? "What gibberish are you speaking? You thought manipulating Marc to bully your niece would what, make it all better? Something is truly wrong in your mind, Royce. You're supposed to be getting better, but I think you're worse. You create your own disaster. This time, you're going to lose your entire family from your lies and behavior. I knew that if I just let you keep on talking, your true self would be revealed. You have a vengeful spirit. I thought we could work it out, but I was mistaken. Be happy in your misery because divorce is coming. I'm done!"

With that, Grayling stormed out, leaving his wife screaming his name. It looked like he was about to be a divorced man. He had no idea she held any contempt towards his sister, and that she would stoop low enough to seek out Strom. She needed her butt beat.

♦ ♦ ♦

Royce couldn't breathe. She wanted to smack herself. She didn't mean to say what she had, but her emotions were off. She hated being in rehab because it was knocking her off her game. She knew that she had pushed Grayling too far, and the only way to get back on his good side was to fix her relationship with her daughter.

She started to smack herself in the head and quietly berated herself for being so stupid. There was no need for her to act out the way she had. All she had to do was play it cool, but to show just how jealous she was of his and Gwen's relationship was wrong. She knew Grayling just loved his little sister and that nothing had ever happened between the two, but she was so angry that he'd sold her out. She wanted to hurt him like she was hurting and had officially screwed herself. She started chanting that she didn't mean it. She didn't want to lose her husband. It was a weakness that had caused her to do what she did, but she never thought she'd get caught, and she never thought Grayling would drop the D-word. She wouldn't survive that. She had to do something.

"Royce," Janice called, holding her hand to keep her from self-abusing herself any longer.

"I know, Janice, I know. There is no reason for you to comment. I messed up," she replied bluntly and got up and left the room with a throbbing headache and wet eyes.

♦ ♦ ♦

"G, you've got to calm down. Now, I've phoned Gwendolyn and asked her to come over," Antwon told him, hoping to calm his friend. The man had been on a warpath ever since he'd left the rehab center.

"I can't believe the audacity of that woman. She knows the monster that Strom is. hen to throw out an unfounded allegation and suggest I would molest or have an incestual relationship with my sister… That was beyond petty, that was downright dirty and cruel. That woman, this woman who I've seen for nearly three months, isn't my wife. This woman is bitter, belligerent and devious. It's like she's the devil's puppet. No wonder my daughter left. Royale saw what I was too naïve and weak to see," he fumed.

Antwon shifted on the couch as Grayling started to pace and mumble. When his friend had called him and told him what was said, he wanted to slap some sense into Royce. She had officially lost her mind and had gone too far. He told Grayling before he married Royce that she wasn't the one. She just wanted to be out of her parents' control.

"She was wrong, man. She ain't had no right to disrespect you like that. I agree and validate your feelings. However, you need to be strong for Royale. With this lawsuit becoming public, the media is on you, so let's just keep a cool head."

"Keep a cool head? She told me it was my fault she was cheating. I mean, who does that? She was talking out the side of her neck. First, I was into my ministry, and that was why she cheated, now she's claiming I'm too into my family, and that's why she had an affair. She's just rotten and bitter."

Before the conversation could go further, there was a knock at the door, and Antwon went to answer it. When he opened the door, Gwendolyn and Rina were standing there. Neither knew the full extent of what was going on. Antwon didn't want to upset them over the phone, but he knew that when G was in this frame of mind, he needed his sister.

"Uncle Antwon, you're here?" Rina asked, offering him a hug and he returned it.

"Hey, sweet girl. How about you go check on Grayling for me? I need to talk to your mom quick."

She gave him an odd look like she knew something was up but didn't question him. Instead, she nodded and walked off, leaving him and Gwendolyn alone. He waited a moment and took Gwendolyn in. He would never understand why Strom had mistreated this goddess of a woman. "Hey, beautiful."

She smiled at him and returned the salutation. He and Gwendolyn had been friends for nearly as long as he had been friends with G, but they had only recently taken their friendship to the next level. However, they hadn't gone public due to all the press the family was getting. Neither of them wanted to add stress to Grayling's already stressful situation, but he was upset that Royce would suggest what Gwen had, and he needed to tell her before she heard it from an angry Grayling.

"I gotta tell you something, and you aren't going to like it. It has to do with your selfish sister-in-law and her extreme pettiness. She's officially off her rocker."

"Tell me now," Gwendolyn requested with a frown.

He spoke as quickly as he could as they walked slowly into the living room where Grayling was still seething. Rina was doing her best to ascertain what was going on, but none of the adults wanted to put her in the middle of the madness.

"Rina, dear, I need to talk to Grayling and Antwon. Can you give us some privacy?"

"Okay," she replied.

♦ ♦ ♦

Rina wasn't as naïve as they believed, and she hated to be treated like a child. It was obvious something had occurred that had greatly impacted the family. Whatever was happening, she could handle it, so instead of leaving, she eavesdropped. Rina was completely unprepared for the tea they were dropping. She couldn't believe her aunt would reach out to Strom, or that she would say those hurtful words to her own husband. Was the woman really that jealous? She shook her head in dismay. Normally, she was the one who was patient and always the peacekeeper, but right now she wanted to give Royce the butt whooping she deserved. Angered, she reached for her cellphone and dialed Royale, who picked up on the second ring.

"Sissy, your vessel has officially lost her mind. She's next level mental. You know I forgive the quickest and seek to find the good in everyone, but she has gone too far. Dad is hurt and livid. Even my mom and Uncle Antwon are pissed off."

"What happened? What did she do?"

"Firstly, she blamed Dad for her affair, claiming he spent more time with my mom and me than he did her. Then she alleged that my mom and your dad were having an incestual relationship. Oh, and the worst part is, she reached out to Strom. That's how Marc found him.

Apparently, she's been contacting him low-key. From what Dad was saying, she told him it was time to forgive. Did she forget what he did to us?"

"You better tell the truth and shame the Devil. How is daddy doing?"

"Not good. I know you're coming home tomorrow after church, but I'm worried, Royale. Your mom's affair is affecting everyone, and she's not even taking responsibility for her actions. To top it all off, Sister Roslyn is suing for defamation of character and pain and suffering."

There was complete silence between the two for nearly ten minutes. The only reason Rina knew Royale was still on the phone was because she heard her breathing.

"I'm coming home now. Daddy can't be alone at a time like this. She had no right to come at him like that. My goodness, what is happening to our family?"

"I don't know, but the sooner you get here, the better. I should go now."

"Okay, Rina. Thank you for informing me of the situation. I love you and I will be home soon, like, real soon."

"Okay, love you too," Rina replied and hung the phone up. Then she quickly got on her knees to pray, because if they ever needed prayer and God's grace, it was at this critical moment. It seemed like it was all getting worse instead of better.

CHAPTER 13

The sound of Christian rapper KB's song "Crowns & Thorns (Oceans)" was playing, the words of the song tugging at Royale's heart. Tears threatened to fall after as she recounted what Rina had told her. So much had happened in such a short time and it was tearing her family apart, ripping at the seams all because Royce was a selfish, narcissistic human being. The sad part was there was something else she had kept hidden, buried so deep she hoped it would never resurface, but she feared it would. If Royce were taking the counseling seriously, then their shared dark secret would soon be told.

Royale silently wondered if her father knew about Royce's *male friends*. That should have been an indicator to Royale that Matan would be susceptible to Royce's advances. What was far worse than that was to imply that Royale's father and his sister were together. How could Royce make such horrid accusations, knowing they were all lies? It burned Royale to her core that the woman who had inflicted so much strife in the family was at it again. If the world wasn't revolving around her, then it wasn't turning. Royce cared nothing about anyone else.

Every fiber in her body wanted to jump into her SUV, drive home and soothe her father. He didn't deserve any of this. She should at least call him, but she didn't know what to say. She wasn't angry anymore, at least not with her father. Honestly, she was never upset with him, she was just hurt and felt abandoned by him. The days since she had left and been with the Byse family and Khan, her bleeding heart wasn't bleeding anymore. She was surrounded by people who loved God, not on the surface where eyes could see, but bone deep. That allowed her to see beyond her own pain. Of course, her father was just as hurt, if not more, after finding out his wife who he adored and raved about was having an affair with his protégé.

As Royale sat quietly, allowing KB's lyrics to weave through her mind, she was suddenly pulled back into time. Her mind wandered, as she sought the moment when she and her mother lost their connection, and finally, she deduced they never had one. Everything was just a façade, and that truth made her emotional.

Royce had always been an actress, and the world her stage. Now that she really thought about it, as much as she loved Royce once, it was never truly returned. Not like Gwendolyn loved Czarina. They had a true mother-daughter bond. Maybe a little too much of an attachment, but it was love. Royale couldn't pinpoint a moment when she had that with Royce. Their attachment was always different, which could explain Royce's lack of decorum.

Royale was so deeply lost in thought she didn't hear the arrival of Khan.

"Royale, are you okay? If you want to go home now, I'll help drive," Khan offered.

A smile formed when she felt his candied dulcet baritone cascade through her flesh, causing her to abandon all thoughts of her past. It was completely maddening how he had that effect on her, but it was a feeling that was becoming addictive. Butterflies, no, more like a flock of geese erupted in her stomach as he rested his thick, calloused hand gently on her shoulder, causing her to lean into him. It was then she got a whiff of the culinary delights Momma Byse was creating. Momma Byse and her husband, Keith, had decided to have an impromptu cookout for Royale since she was departing tomorrow. They were fixing her favorites like shrimp bacon ranch pasta salad, Bush's baked beans, barbecue chicken, turkey burgers, and turkey hotdogs with all the fixings. If only she could bottle up this moment and take it with her.

Sighing softly, she turned around and watched with enthused eyes as Khan sat down beside her. He was a handsome man, like, so handsome she would never think he would give her a second thought, and now she couldn't go a second without thinking about him.

He wore a button up Ralph Lauren plaid shirt and 501 original Levi jeans that were cuffed, showcasing his Steve Madden Harpoon Derby shoes. He looked model perfect in anything he wore. They'd both cleaned up nicely after the hike and grabbed a bite to eat at Chipotle Mexican Grill, which was her favorite place to eat. She was still full from the chicken bowl she'd ordered and wondered how she was going to eat the feast that was being cooked now.

Looking at him, she wondered why she hadn't met Khan first, but then shook the idea. God's timing was perfect timing. The more time she spent with Khan, the more she realized he was worth waiting for. "I appreciate the offer, but I'll leave first thing in the morning," she told him as she reached out to hold his hand.

She observed him looking at her, his eyes taking in her honey copper ones. He smiled as he openly gaped at her fitted dress and his eyes finally rested on her ring. Before he could ask, she gave an explanation. "This is a ring my dad bought Rina and me. He said that any man interested in me needed to go to my Father before he could have my hand and heart. I haven't been wearing it since everything went down, but it feels right to wear it now."

Khan smiled. "Your dad is a wise man. If a man doesn't have a heart for Christ, then what good is he to lead a family when he only worships himself? Don't worry, I'm talking to the Father, and I'll be talking to your earthly father as soon as you feel ready. August is coming sooner than later, and I want us to be official in some capacity. I know once you start your graduate courses the men with come flocking, and I'm not having that." He gave her his most charming grin.

She reached up and caressed his cheek. She loved feeling connected to him in some way, and she wasn't sure how she'd handle not seeing him daily. However, they had promised each other they'd talk on the phone, FaceTime and Skype. It wouldn't be the same, but she wanted to handle her past so she could enjoy her present and build her future. A future she had given up on just a few months ago until Khan rekindled her dying embers and gave her hope once more.

"I agree. Just let me talk to my dad and see where his head is. I'd like to get closure with Matan as well. When I leave home to start over in Philadelphia, Pennsylvania, I don't want my past coming back to haunt me. I want all the blessings God has in store for me, and I need to leave the drama. I want to make sure you have the best of me, not broken pieces," she shared.

"That sounds like a plan, but just to let you know, I'll accept your broken pieces because we can heal together. We'll be stronger. You can trust me with all the parts of you. I don't just want best, I want every single morsel that is you," he told her.

Royale blushed, as usual, but leaned over to kiss his cheek. "I almost think you're too good to be true."

"No, it's just that now you're dealing with a man and no longer an immature boy," he countered and kissed her back.

"Agreed," she replied before shifting the conversation. "Oh, next Saturday, are you going to see Mr. Giles? If so, I'll come back Friday night, so I can be there to support you," she offered, her fingers toying with his unbound blonde strands.

"Thank you, but I don't want you in a prison. I'd end up locked up myself if anyone looked at you the wrong way. I know you forget this, but you are famous, not to mention gorgeous. People do recognize you, and I wouldn't react well if someone spoke out of turn to you."

Royale nodded. "I can be there when it's over. I just feel like it's a huge deal and you should have all the support you can get. I want you to know I'm here. I want to be there for you."

He smiled. "I don't know where you've been all my life, but I know for sure now that you're here, I'm not letting you go. It means a lot that you care so much. We'll figure it out later. Let's get your family situation in order and then we can deal with mine."

"Deal."

"Lovebirds, the food is ready!" Canton yelled.

They nodded in unison and prepared to fix their plates.

◆ ◆ ◆

The house was too quiet, and his mind was too loud. All Grayling did was replay what had happened between him and his wife. He never thought it would be this way. Unable to sleep, he leaned over to turn on his iHome and the sounds of Isaac Carree's song "Clean This House" hummed through the bedroom, and instantly, tears connected under Grayling's chin. He needed God to clean his house, heart, and head. He felt like he was drowning in depression and deceit.

His mind was full of *what ifs*, and *whys*. Rest and sleep had evaded him, and he thought playing the music would help lift the burden that seemed to be suffocating him, but he was unable to find the peace he sought. To further add insult to injury, Royce had called his cellphone and landline, more than likely to plead her case, but it was a futile effort. He ignored her. Her words and allegations wounded him in a way that would take years to heal. That was the hard part about loving a person and becoming one with them: they knew all of your weaknesses and how to exploit them. They knew right where to strike the death blow.

Sighing in frustration, he yanked the duvet off and grabbed his Bible that was sitting on the nightstand and made his way to his prayer closet. If he had to pray until his knees bled, he would. Something had to give. He wasn't this man. He didn't shout or grow weary; he didn't give in or give up. He stayed prayed up, but ever since the betrayal of his wife, he felt less than. He felt exposed and weak. It was impacting his daily walk in Christ, and that couldn't happen.

He entered his warrior room, shut the door behind him and dropped to his knees. Nothing. He couldn't form the words to pray, but his heart was full, so he wept. He let it out. All the insecurity, anger, fear and pain flowed until finally, he could cry no more and he started to cry out to God. His prayer was raw, and at times inaudible, but he knew God understood. He pleaded in the name of Jesus to have the hardness in his heart removed and to love and see how God love and sees, and mostly, to treat others not as they have treated him, but how God treats all His children. He prayed to be strong enough to endure the storm that was brewing and replace fear with faith. He mourned over his actions toward his daughter and asked for forgiveness in how he had reacted to both Royale and Royce. Lastly, he asked God to heal the hurt. He was deeply wounded. He was so hurt by Matan and Royce, he wanted their pain and shame to equal his own, and he knew that was a worldly ideology and not a Godly one. He had to let go. If Hosea could take a prostitute as a wife, if God could forgive David for his actions and all others, then he could find a way to get through the storm he was facing with his wife. He would have to forgive Royce, but forgiveness didn't equal togetherness. Finally, he ended his prayer and lamentation with, "Teach me how to love, to pray and to forgive as You, Father."

Feeling renewed and refreshed, he hummed a hymn the ladies used to sing in church when he was a boy. *"Talk about me as much as you please, and I'll talk about you down on my knees, as long as I know I got a seat in the kingdom that's all right."* At the end of the day, he was living to hear God say, *"Well done,"* and to not spew him out for being lukewarm. He had to trust in God and let it all go.

After his prayer and praise session, he walked back to his bedroom, placed his Bible down and asked God to allow his daughter safe passage home and to grant him a good night's sleep. Now was the time to give everything he had to get his family back on track. He was the head of the household, and his family wouldn't fail under his watch.

CHAPTER 14

The darkness intruded like a thief, arousing Momma Byse out of a soundless sleep. Holding her breath for a moment, her small ears perked up, sensing that something was off. Slowly, she removed her warmed body and sought to find what was assaulting her mind. All day, ever since Royale had explained that she had to go home, something hadn't been sitting well in her spirit.

Later that evening, after they had all eaten, she noticed how close Royale and Khan had become and it alarmed her. Not because she didn't want the pair to be happy together, but because she knew the type of man, or lack of man, Ronald was. She knew what he was capable of. He was a man without morals, without God, without respect for life.

Shaking the thoughts, she eased away from her husband and slid her legs off the bed. Her bare feet hit the wooden floor below, and in doing so, it was like she had tripped a silent alarm as she felt her husband's body shift in the bed, seeking her, only to find emptiness and sheets.

"What's going on, Nina?" Keith's hoarse voice asked.

She turned slowly, her dark eyes met his intense, captivating emerald eyes that seemed to brighten in the darkness. It was a family gene that had skipped both her children.

"My spirit is telling me something isn't right, and I want to check on the children and make sure everything is okay. I can't put a finger on it, but I just feel like God is warning me," she confessed to him.

"Now I see why you made all the boys spend the night. Nina Bear, don't go fretting about what we have already taken to God in prayer. Come on back to bed, it seems like a lifetime since I held you. Them grown children will be fine."

She smiled at him but shook her head. Yes, they had prayed and would again this morning before she allowed Royale to travel, but still, something didn't feel right. "Keith, just let me go see about them so my spirit can settle, then I'll come right back to bed."

"Right back, wife."

She nodded in agreement, then left out the bedroom.

♦ ♦ ♦

On his way home with two flunkies and Hoss, Ronald decided to drive by where he knew Khan was staying and was surprised to not find his truck. So he and his crew drove by Nina Byse's house and saw a slew of vehicles, one being his son's. Maybe it was the alcohol, or maybe it was just pent up anger, but Ronald went into a mental rage. Khan thought he could really be disrespectful and pay no consequences for his actions. Well, he would learn today. He would feel his father's wrath.

Even in his drunken state, he knew exactly what to do. He told Hoss to call the others and have them meet him. He was no longer playing around. He could see now that Nina didn't know how to mind her business. Had she never found her way back into his son's life, the boy wouldn't be a lover of those inferiors. No son of his would continue to side with the enemy. He tried to beat that soft spot for the darkies out of him, but his wife had instilled it deeply.

Years ago, when he was on the police force and his wife met that woman, Nina Byse, it was the start of the ending of his precious wife and lovely life. They were at the flea market, both interested in the same item, and Nina told Khloe she could have it. By the time they found Khan, he had become fast friends with Nina's son, Nehemiah. There began his wife's friendship with that woman. No matter what he did or said, Nina and Khloe just got closer until closer caused death. Now it looked like the same might happen to his son.

"Your boy needs to be reminded of where he came from. I know his momma was friendly with them, but we ain't. I say we send a message, especially after what Everleigh said about that muddy filling in for Ms. Judy giving her lip."

"I agree."

♦ ♦ ♦

Royale slowly unfolded her body. Sleep had not come easy, even after Momma Byse had prayed. Something in her spirit wouldn't allow her to relax. Before she went to bed, close to midnight, she texted Rina to make sure the family was okay. When she confirmed they were, it was only then that her eyes closed, but it was a fitful slumber, one that caused her to awake two hours later to make sure the Byse family, Khan, and his cousin were all okay. They were. Now at six in the morning, she was peeling herself out of bed and getting ready to return home to face the pain she had avoided for so long.

She picked up her clothing and headed to the shower to take care of her hygiene, and as soon as she opened the door, she heard scrambling of feet and screaming. Her body kicked into high gear without knowing why. She followed the shouting downstairs, only to find Momma Byse standing with the front door open, wearing her house gown open, her hand over her heart and shaking her head. She was calling to Kisha to come back inside while the men were outside. To get a better look, she walked behind Momma Byse and saw what the fuss was about. Four stuffed scarecrows were hanging from the large oak tree in the yard, each having a member of the Byse family's name on it.

"My Lord. Who would do something like that?" Royale asked out loud, not really seeking an answer, but surprised by what she saw. Did people still actually do that?

"Momma, I called the police," Kisha informed.

"Okay, baby, but nothing will come of it," she replied as she watched the four men cut down the offensive warning. Then she turned to Royale. "The people who did this are full of pure hatred, full of jealous rage and completely insecure. People like this have weak minds and even weaker hearts. This kind of person or persons who commit these cowardly acts under the guise of the night are the worst kind of offenders, but I'll counter their hate with God's love. C'mon so I can feed you before you go. I want Khan and them to follow you out so I know you'll be safe."

"Yes, ma'am."

Royale felt like she was missing a lot. Something told her that Momma Byse knew who had committed this heinous act and that it might have to do with Khan. The wounded look of distress in his eyes made her wonder just how deeply his father's hatred ran. Was he capable of this, and if so, what other things was he capable of?

Biting her lower lip to calm her anxiety, Royale turned back inside the house and sat quietly at the kitchen table. Her SUV had been repacked the night before. Khan and the others reloaded it properly and did an inspection of her vehicle to make sure it was ready for the ride back to Virginia. She was nervous about returning home, but that was blown out of the water when two police officers arrived and Mr. Byse greeted them and started to explain what had happened. He also pulled out his cellphone to show the picture since they had cut down the hanging scarecrows.

Still quiet in thought, Royale could feel Khan's arrival. He was always a force and feeling him near had brought her a feeling of solace and safety, but right now, his presence wasn't helping. Right now, her mind was clouded, and she was worried about what this meant, not just for the Byse family, but for her and Khan.

"Royale, hey, look at me," Khan requested.

She did. There was no way she could ignore the emotion in his voice. However, his request didn't halt her heart palpitations. He reached out and placed his hand gently under her chin. "Are you okay?"

"I'm fine," she replied too quickly and instantly knew her mistake. The squint of his eyes and the tapering of his lips let her know that, and she quickly tried to correct her statement. It wasn't her intention to worry him or lie to him. "I mean, I'll be fine. It was just a shock. Did…did your father do this?"

He exhaled a heavy breath. "I don't know. Don't worry about that now. I just want to make sure you are okay. I don't want you having an anxiety attack on me."

Before she could say anything, they were interrupted by a subdued Nehemiah.

"Khan, it's the fire station on the phone, your business was set on fire. They were able to contain it, so it's not a total loss, but they need you there. They think it's arson," Nehemiah explained.

Royale looked at Khan with concerned but fearful eyes. She quickly noted how the color drained from his golden, sun-kissed face and his eyes closed. She knew without it being confirmed that his father had not only sent a threat to the Byse family, but also to his own son, and that pissed her off. She wasn't going to have an anxiety attack, but she was going to have Khan's back. "Go, Khan, I'm fine. I'll call you hourly until I get home."

"Royale."

"No, Khan, I'll be fine. I'm not having an anxiety attack. I promise. Now go," she instructed. After a moment, he nodded and left with Canton right behind him.

Thirty minutes later, Royale was headed out. Mr. and Mrs. Byse prayed for her to travel safely and she was off. She called Ma Gwendolyn to let her know she was starting out and would call, updating her when she was closer to home. Just like when she left Virginia to come to West Virginia, her heart was heavy. She was concerned about Khan's welfare and the side effects of a parental betrayal. She prayed for him. No longer were she and Khan living a fairytale; they were now dealing with the real world. Would they survive it if his father was that set on getting revenge on his own son? Would Khan leave and deceive her as Matan had done? Had she run from one failure to another? No. Khan wasn't Matan and she could trust him, couldn't she?

By hour two, she had spoken to Khan four times, and her anxiety had greatly decreased, as did her unfounded worry. Khan had a warrior's heart, and he wasn't going to allow the ignorance of another to control his life. That was what she liked about him, his fighting spirit, which was what she needed now too. If he could stand up to his father, it was time for her to stand up to her mother. It was time to tell everything. No longer did she care about how Royce felt. The truth would set her free, and she longed for freedom.

CHAPTER 15

Matan and his friends had the most eventful trip in the short time they were in Las Vegas. They gambled, and Matan won three thousand dollars and was smart enough to stop gambling after that. He needed that money in his 'just in case' fund. His boys, Tataya and Charles, weren't so lucky, and Fontaine and Maurice were smart enough not to gamble at all. Then they went indoor skydiving and did the dream racing experience, which was epic. Just like Fontaine had predicted, he felt better, well, until now. Now, he was mentally cursing himself for answering the phone. As soon as he said hello, he wanted to say goodbye.

"Don't hang up, Matan, it's Royce. Just listen to me, please. I'm in a treatment facility, and part of my treatment is to reach out to those I have hurt during my sickness. I've spoken to my husband and parents, and I would like to talk to you."

"I have nothing to say to you, and you have nothing to say to me. Your actions after what happened were enough for me. Please don't call me again." He hung up, blocked the number and let out a sigh. He just wanted her to leave him alone. The last person she needed to be contacting was him.

He dialed his mother, knowing it was late back home, or early, but he knew she would put Royce in her place.

"Who this?" the sleep-filled voice answered.

"Momma, it's me. Royce just called me, and I hung up on her. She said that part of her treatment is to reach out to the people she hurt. Can you deal with her? My only concern is getting back with Royale and distancing myself from her mother."

"Boy, where you at? You got some nerve calling me now when I've been calling all over the world looking for you."

Well, it seemed his mom was wide awake now, but she was right. After talking to his father, he had been ignoring his mom. "I'm in Vegas. I needed new scenery. I'll be back Monday morning. I'm sorry about not returning your calls, it's just that my mind has been all over the place."

"Yeah, well mine has been too. We need to talk. I'll go see about Royce. I know where she is. My friend girl works at the rehab facility she's in. I heard her and Grayling got into a big argument and that Royale is coming back to Virginia, so don't act no fool in Vegas."

"Okay, momma. Thank you. I love you."

"Yeah, I bet you do. Acting all ungrateful until you need me to clean up your mess. Get off my line!" Then, she hung up the phone on him.

◆ ◆ ◆

Weary, nearly to the point of exhaustion, Royale pulled into her father's driveway. It had been a long, tedious, but revealing and thought-provoking ride. The entire nine weeks had gone through her head while she drove herself home. She hadn't thought of her father's house as home in a long time.

Tears fell down the slopes of her apple cheeks, and she rested her head on the steering wheel. Memories of a life-long past ran through her mind like a movie reel. Releasing a heavy sigh, she let out the anger she held against her father. Their first introduction had been so violent because neither had spoken about what Royce had done, or how her actions had impacted them. Instead, they both took their frustration out on each other. She wouldn't do that now.

She looked in the mirror, her reflection a beautiful melding of both her parents. She was thankful to not have inherited her vessel's cruel, narcissistic ways. She cleaned herself up and allowed her coloring to get back to normal before she opened the door and forced her stiff body out of the car, and gingerly gaited toward the front door.

Royale wasn't sure what she was going to say to her father, and for the first time, she wondered if he were even home. It was Sunday afternoon, and he was probably at church. She put her key in the door and unlocked it, and for some reason, her heartbeat increased. Possibly out of fear of how she would be received by her father if he were home. Before she could pull the key out, the door was pulled opened and her father pulled her into a deep embrace. Like a lost child, she melted into him, needing him more than she realized.

"Royale, please forgive me my trespasses against you. I didn't mean to hit you, and I've been breaking ever since I did that," he implored as he peppered kisses atop her head.

"It's okay, daddy. I'm sorry too," she replied in a childlike voice as she burrowed deeper into his embrace. The scent of Dove men calmed her wariness. It was so good to be home. She missed this. She missed him. "I thought when I left that you were siding with her and that you'd tell me I had to forgive her and let it go. I thought you blamed me. I was so dazed, broken and apprehensive. I didn't know what to do, so I ran."

"I know, baby. I know," he cooed as he pulled back and looked her over to make sure she was okay. "Come on inside so we can talk. Later, the family will come by, but for now, you and I need each other. I think we're the only two who understands how the other feels. So, let's have the conversation we should have had nine weeks ago."

Two hours later, tears dried, feelings repaired, the two shared a meal. Royale was livid with Marc and her vessel. It upset her how far her vessel had gone, and she feared she was going to have to break her father's heart more. He had been through a lot, more than she had thought, and it troubled her that he was doing it without her support. Now she had to tell him the other part.

"Daddy, I have something to tell you, and I don't know how you're going to feel. However, I want no lies or anything left unsaid between us. Royce hasn't been completely honest with you, or she can't count."

Grayling gave his daughter a perplexed look. "What are you talking about?"

She bit her bottom lip to gather the strength she needed because honestly, the last thing she ever wanted to do was make her father suffer more agony, but he deserved the truth, no matter how ugly it was. "You said she told you she had emotional affairs for nine years before she started her sexual affair with Matan, which would suggest I was about thirteen when it all started—that's just untrue. It started earlier than that. I remember some of them, her friends, she called them. I started ballet and contemporary dance when I was six, right?"

"Yes."

"That's about the time it started. She met Braden, then there was Jeffery, and my least favorite, Leering Larry. She dropped him because he paid more attention to me than her. After that, she made sure I didn't meet her friends anymore."

"Leering Larry?" he queried.

Without looking at her father, she simply nodded before speaking. "She met him at the park. He always made me feel uncomfortable."

"Sweetheart…" He paused, closing his eyes as if he were trying to think of the best way to ask the question, he wanted her to answer. She didn't need to be clairvoyant to know what her father was contemplating. "Why did he make you feel uncomfortable?"

"It was years ago, daddy."

"Please tell me," he stated with urgency.

Instantly, goosebumps popped out on her arm. Royale looked everywhere to avoid his intuitive stare. She could feel his panic and fear. It overtook the entire room, almost suffocating her. She licked her lips and took three deep breaths. Her anxiety wanted to rear its ugly head, but she fought against it. She never thought she would ever have to tell him about that. It wasn't as bad as it could have been, but it still shouldn't have occurred.

"Royale Makeda Chastain, please tell me."

Her tear ducts were dry now; there were no tears to fall. She exhaled and shared with him what her mother had made her bury deep in her mind. So deeply, Royale wondered if what she recalled was fact or fiction. "I…he…it was all so innocent," she started as her mind went back to the past, she hadn't thought about in years but was still enslaved to. Somewhere deep within that unhealed wound still caused her pain. Pulling her long hair into a messy ponytail, she continued. "He would push me on the swing and give me treats. It started to feel strange when he would put me on his knee and whisper in my ear."

"Did he rape you?" Grayling asked in a whisper.

There was a pregnant pause. The tension quickly filled the room, making it feel much smaller than it was. Royale knew her father would eradicate Larry if he could. At that moment, being a bishop didn't matter. He was and would always be a father, and fathers protected their daughters at all cost.

"No, I'm still a virgin." She heard her father let out a sigh of relief. She hoped the next part wouldn't upset him too much. "However, he touched me in places he shouldn't have. The day he tried to take it to that level, Mom walked in. She defended me, but then blamed me all at once. It was weird. I remember she yanked me off the bed so hard, her sable eyes widened with disgust and fury. She screamed at him, and he swore it was me who had started it. Me, like at seven I somehow knew how to seduce a man. I didn't even know what he was doing, all I knew was that I was terrified and wanted it to stop." She let out a humorless chuckle before continuing.

"Then she told me not to tell you about it or her other friends. She said you would kill Larry and be taken from me and your soul would be damned to hell. She said it just like that, and I believed her. It was why when Strom was beating on Ma Gwendolyn, Czarina and I kept it secret. I didn't want to lose you. I kept those secrets to keep you. I wanted her and I to be connected, but she discarded me instead. I felt so bad, alone and used. Then I just willed myself to forget. I buried it deep, and when it tried to come back up, I pushed it deeper until there was no place for it to go. Of course, seeing her with Matan brought it all back, which is probably what set off my anxiety attacks." She sniffled as the invisible tears clung to her body. No longer did she have to keep those horrid moments secret. Her father knew, and the world hadn't ended.

"I'm sorry, Royale. I should have known. You know that none of this was your fault. I don't want you feeling shame about any of this past or present. Royce was wrong to place you in danger and wrong to place blame on you. Lord knows I'm so sorry I let it happen to you."

She could hear the cry in his voice and it nearly undid her. His strong baritone was reduced to a quivering mess. He was hurting, too, but he wanted to be strong for her. She knew he blamed himself for not knowing and not protecting her, but she didn't want him to place that needless guilt on himself. "You were building your church. I don't blame you, and you have no reason to feel guilty. There're girls in our church who have survived far worse than what happened to me, and you helped them. Look at what Ma Gwendolyn and Rina survived."

"Don't do that, Royale. Don't minimize what you suffered. That night when Strom nearly beat Gwendolyn to death, he attacked you too. That's twice in your life I wasn't there when you needed me." He shook his head, as if trying to clear his thoughts. "That should have never happened, and Royce shouldn't have kept that from me. You must have been so frightened and confused. You were just seven. My Lord, how had I missed it?"

"She had to, because if she told you, then she would have to tell it all. I'm sure she wanted the Larry incident to go with her to her grave. Honestly, I'm not even mad about that. I got through it. One day, I'll get over what she and Matan did, but I can't get over her accusing you of what she did, or her reaching out to Strom via Marc. She's just trying to deflect from her own sins. Lord knows we all have to answer for our sins, so why does she think she's exempt?"

"Royale, I never knew you were carrying so much torment. At seven, you were sexually accosted by a man your mother was having an emotional affair with, then two years later, you were nearly killed by Strom when he stabbed you. Goodness, I've failed you in so many ways.

"You have my word from this day forward, I'll not fail you again. I never want you to feel like you can't come to me and I'll do everything in my power to be the father you always need. Please forgive me for not being there and not listening. Your mother was right about one thing: maybe I put too much ahead of my family."

Royale reached out her hand and clasped it with her father's. No words were spoken, they just let God's peace and love envelop them. His presence was there.

◆ ◆ ◆

Grayling watched over his daughter protectively as she slumbered effortlessly in her Olympic queen bed. His heart felt whole to have her home. He had prayed unceasingly after his daughter had confessed a nearly decade and a half old secret to him. It fragmented his heart that Royale had been holding on to something so atrocious all because she wanted her mother's acceptance and love.

Royce had manipulated Royale by playing on her fears that he would abandon his family. All Royale wanted was a connection with her mother. He truly had no idea who Royce was. It was one thing to curse him and throw away their marriage—he viewed that as an attack on him—but to violate their daughter, to betray her innocence in that way and to insinuate that Royale was to blame for a grown man committing lewd and lascivious acts against her unblemished flesh was too much. It was a deception he could not dismiss. That was an act that only God's intervention could force him to forgive. Right now, he wanted to beat the black off Royce, and only the love of his girls kept him from doing so.

"God, please don't allow evil hands to touch my daughter again. She has suffered in ways I'll never be able to understand, but God, give me the words and actions to help her feel safe, loved and treasured again. Let my love be enough to cover the lack of love her mother never gave her. Heal her hurt, Father. Please heal my heart, so I act in love and not in anger. In Jesus' name, amen."

As he finished the prayer, his daughter's cellphone started ringing again. He looked at the ID, but the name and number were unknown to him. Who was Prince Charming? He'd ask later. Right now, he just wanted her to rest. He had reached out to the family to let them know she had arrived home safely and he knew they would be arriving after church.

♦ ♦ ♦

Khan left another voicemail for Royale. He assumed she was sleeping and that she would call him as soon as she was able, he just wanted to hear her voice.

"Did she answer?" Canton queried, concerned.

"No. I think she's sleeping. She's had a long day."

"Yeah, she did have a long ride. Plus, you called her like a hundred times," Canton teased.

Khan wanted to smile, but he was too upset. Not about Royale, but about how his father had chosen to seek revenge. There was a lot of damage at his business, but it was fully covered by insurance. His father was an idiot. He had cameras all around his business, so he knew it was the Knight Ryders who had torched his building. He made sure to send a copy to the police. He was also sure his father had left the scarecrows hanging at the Byse residence. It was a message, and he had gotten it loud and clear. Because Khan had refused to become his father, Ronald had chosen to come after the people he loved, his family, but he still would not yield to his father's thirst for violence and hate.

Instead, Khan and Canton attended church with the Byse family and prayed. Momma Byse always said there was power in prayer, and he prayed hard. However, for now, he was done with his father. Their relationship had always been iffy, but now it was nonexistent. Ronald had gone too far when he came after the Byse family. He wasn't concerned about the business because he was willing to relocate and rebuild elsewhere, but coming after a family who loved him when his father chose not to was more than he was willing to accept. Ronald would pay.

"Khan, are you okay?" Nehemiah asked.

"I am. How are you? We both know that Ronald and his band of racist brothers are behind this."

"I'm mad, but I know not to sin in anger. He wants attention, so we're going to ignore him and move forward."

"You bros are better than me. I believe in Texas Justice. I say give unto him what he has given to us," Canton insisted.

"Nah, hate begets hate, violence begets violence, and to stop the cycle, somebody has to be like Jesus. Somebody has to be responsible and humble enough to stop the foolery," Nehemiah philosophized.

"I love Jesus too. All I'm saying is, there is a time for everything and Uncle Ronald has gone too far now. That was a threat, a real threat, and I don't appreciate it. Khan, I think you should consider moving your business to Texas. There's no reason for you to stay in West Virginia."

Khan never had been and never would be a runner. He wasn't leaving West Virginia until he settled what he needed to settle with his father and got his mother justice.

"I'll rebuild my business, that's not a problem. What I won't do is run with my tail stuck between my legs. Ronald doesn't run me, and I won't be moved. I'm going to keep a low profile, get some security for Momma Byse, and find out what's going on with the Giles situation.

I'm not going to give Ronald another thought. Let's eat. I know Momma Byse is done with the cooking.

CHAPTER 16

Roslyn had her hair pulled into a high ponytail, at forty-five, she looked twenty-nine and still had a banging body because she stayed in shape. At five feet five, she was petite and curvy, and everybody told her she favored Toni Braxton. For the life of her, she didn't know why Grayling left her for Royce's unfaithful, slutty self, but she wasn't giving up on him. Royce just gave her more than enough ammunition to use to enact her plan of getting Grayling back.

Basically, after Matan informed her that Royce was reaching out to him, she was more than happy to set her straight. There would be no more playing it nice; they were going to have the fallout of all fallouts. Roslyn parked her car and got out, heading to the rehab center. She wanted to laugh. How in the heck had Royce convinced Grayling that she was a sex addict when in all honesty, she was just an old-school slut bucket? She would uncover that soon enough.

She crossed her leg while waiting on Royce's arrival. She knew that Royce wouldn't turn her away when she came for a visit. They had a long rival that would never end until Roslyn got Grayling back.

"Wow, you didn't have to dress up for me," Royce sneered as she walked around to stand in front of Roslyn.

"This is my normal attire. You, on the other hand, look a bit disheveled. I guess having Grayling abandon you has really had a negative impact," Roslyn insulted.

"Aww, are you still hot about me getting him?" she inquired and bent down to get in Roslyn's ear. "He's still my husband, and no matter what I do, he'll never come back to you."

Roslyn snapped her neck and almost spat all in Royce's face, but calmed her temperament. She came here on a mission, and she needed to complete it. Instead of being sucked into the game that Royce was playing, she just laughed it off. They both knew between the two of them, Royce was bad with her mouth, but Roslyn was bad with her fist. She could lay Royce out with no problem, but those days were behind her, or so she hoped.

She cleared her throat. "I'm sure the divorce papers are in the works, so he should be single soon. Now, back up out my face, your breath is kicking harder than a soccer player." At the scornful snub, Roslyn watched with satisfaction as Royce backed away from her and sat down like she should have done before. "Now, I came here to you woman to woman to ask you ever so nicely to stop all communication with my son. He called me letting me know that you were harassing him again. We will be seeking a restraining order to stop this barrage of phone calls. He's done with you and doing his best to get his life back on track and get Royale back. It's sad that a woman of your age is so hung up on a young man just starting out in life."

"I haven't been bombarding him with phone calls. I don't want your son. He's played his part, and I'm done with him. If anything, he should be thanking me for teaching him how to sex a grown woman. Please believe he got nothing on Grayling, but you wouldn't know about that because it was me who turned Gray out. You were just some tattered, hood chick with loose lips above and below," she smirked.

Knowing what she was insinuating, Roslyn jumped to her feet, forgetting all about where she was and tried to choke Royce out. Before she could get her hands on her like she wanted to, someone was pulling her off and shouting.

"Stop it! Oh. My. Gosh. She's pregnant! What is wrong with you?" Janice exclaimed, glaring at a surprised Roslyn.

"Janice!" Royce snapped, gasping for air.

"What?" Roslyn asked, shocked. "You pregnant? What'cha tired, old tail doing pregnant? Who is your baby daddy? Is it your husband or my son?" She shook her head in disbelief. The nerve of this heffa. "You talk about me having loose lips? Gal, you're a nasty one." Then, she burst into laughter. "It's official, I just got my man back. Bye, boo!" With that, Roslyn walked off, not believing her good fate.

As soon as Roslyn got back into her Volvo, she called her son and he answered on the first ring.

"Hey, Ma."

"Hey, son. I just came back from talking to Royce and she won't be a problem. But hey, I need to ask you something."

"Ma'am?"

"When you were with her, did you always use a condom?"

"Most of the time, why? She got the clap or something?"

She could hear the fear in his voice. "No, fool, she's pregnant. Most likely, your dumb tail is the daddy. Now you really done did it. I can't fix this."

"Nah, Ma, ain't no way. How a woman her age still dropping eggs? If she's pregnant, which I suspect she isn't, then it ain't my baby. It can't be, God wouldn't do that to me."

"Uh, no, you don't get to blame God. You the one who wanted to go excavating in them ancient walls and now you going to be connected to that woman forever. I'm sorry, son, but it looks like you won't ever get Royale back, but there is one happy ending."

"What?"

"I'm getting Grayling Chastain back!" she retorted giddily before she hung up.

To be continued.

Dear Readers,

Thank you for reading my book. I hope you have enjoyed it, and if so, please leave a review. I appreciate all the feedback. Love y'all!

CONTACT INFORMATION

Email: Authorydeonna@gmail.com

IG: @bluetygrezz
Twitter: @CrownedRuby
Facebook: fb.me/Authorydeonna

www.ingramcontent.com/pod-product-compliance
Lightning Source LLC
Chambersburg PA
CBHW050819180626
46814CB00004B/1356